ATLANTASTAN 3

CHRIS GREEN

URBAN AINT DEAD PRESENTS

STAY UP TO DATE

To stay up to date on new releases, plus get information on contests, sneak peeks and more,

Click the link below...
https://mailchi.mp/6d21003686d1/subscribe

SOUNDTRACKS

Scan the QR Code below to listen to the Soundtracks/Singles of some of your favorite U.A.D titles:

Don't have Spotify or Apple Music?
No Sweat!
Visit your choice streaming platform and search URBAN AINT DEAD.

Currently on lock serving a bid?
JPay, iHeartRadio, WHATEVER!
We got you covered.
Simply log into your facility's kiosk or tablet, go to music and search
URBAN AINT DEAD.

URBAN AINT DEAD PRESENTS

Like & Follow us on social media:

FB - URBAN AINT DEAD

IG: @uadpresents

Tik Tok - @uadpresents

Submission Guidelines

Submit the first three chapters of your completed manuscript to
urbanaintdead@gmail.com, subject line: Your book's title. The
manuscript must be in a .doc file and sent as an attachment. The
document should be in Times New Roman, double-spaced, and in size
12 font. Also, provide your synopsis and full contact information. If
sending multiple submissions, they must each be in a separate email.
Have a story but no way to submit it electronically? You can still
submit to URBAN AINT DEAD. Send in the first three chapters,
written or typed, of your completed manuscript to:

URBAN AINT DEAD
P.O Box 448
Maybrook, NY 12543

DO NOT send original manuscript. Must be a duplicate.
Provide your synopsis and a cover letter containing your full contact
information.
Thanks for considering URBAN AINT DEAD.

PROLOGUE

Brooklyn New York
Zeus

As I made my way toward my father's meeting room, I couldn't help but notice the weight of the moment. Gathered inside were all the key figures who played a role in our family's operations – men I had grown up calling uncles along with others who shared close ties to our bloodline. Though I wasn't born Italian, my adoptive mother and father embraced me as if I were their own flesh and blood, ensuring I never felt like an outsider in our world.

I never intended to be part of the family business. I didn't choose this life. It was something I was born into and raised around. Tradition ran deep, and my father made sure his values and expectations shaped my path from the very beginning. The lines between family, loyalty, and duty blurred early on, and while I sometimes wondered what my life might have been like outside of this world, it hardly seemed like there had ever been another option for me. The word was that a close relative was murdered down in Atlanta on business relations, and he wanted answers.

"So, what the fuck have any one of you pricks found out about my nephew? It's been longer than forty-eight hours!" my father asked impatiently.

One of his trusted men stepped forward with an unpleasant expression written on his face before speaking.

"Boss, word is he was associated with a guy named Rude Boy and this woman, Taki or Takey. Supposedly, she is the reason for the recent disturbances in their city. A cunt with power. There was also word of him infiltrating, or attempting to infiltrate, the Cubans in Georgia, so the mix-up of his casualty would be from that."

"What mix-up are you talking about? My nephew isn't Cuban; he's a hundred percent Italian. That's my brother's firstborn!" My father's voice was a thunderous growl, reverberating off the walls of the dimly lit office. His eyes blazed with fury, fueled by a protective instinct that ran deep. "Yazi is a don. No one from our bloodline gets touched by outsiders without our say-so. I want every last one of them dead – without exception. Anyone connected to his death should be clocking in on a nine-to-five schedule with their life!"

As his rage filled the room, the tension was palpable. The loyal henchmen surrounding my father shifted uncomfortably, casting glances at one another, their expressions a mix of anxiety and approval. They had seen this side of him before; his wrath could be fierce, but his loyalty was unyielding.

My heart raced; the mention of my uncle and cousin made it all too real. Although I had yet to meet Yazi, family was family, and blood bound us, no matter the distance.

"Don't worry about it, Pop. I'll take care of it," I asserted, stepping forward and folding my arms defiantly.

"No," he replied, his glare sharp enough to cut through the tension. "You need to be here to protect the family. Those Sicilians are planning something unsavory in response to this mess. I need you on the front lines."

"Yes, I am going to handle it," I insisted firmly. "I'll make my way back after I take care of business. It's just a three-day vacation. I'll assemble a team, hunt down the person responsible, and that'll be the end of it."

He struggled with the frustration of my insistence, wanting to deny me the chance to confront this threat. Yet, he knew all too well that I had earned my place at this table, irrespective of his attempts to shield me from the life we led. Business was business, and I was determined to act.

"Fine," he finally relented, his voice still laced with fierce authority. "Eliminate them all. Capish?"

"Capish. I'll be home by Wednesday for supper. We'll head out in the morning," I assured him, the resolve in my voice unwavering.

I surveyed the loyal men around us, some I had known as uncles my entire life. Their support and approval were evident in their nods, a silent reinforcement of my commitment to the family. I was always vigilant when it came to our bloodline, and this mission to the south held more weight than just family business; it was deeply personal.

As I turned on my heel to exit the office, my mind swirled with thoughts of the streets of Harlem, a realm where I was no mere player but a god. In this domain, I answered the disrespect shown to the Blackstar family, delivering consequences when necessary. Now, my resolve would transform into action, and I was ready to hunt down those who dared to challenge our lineage. The time for retribution had come.

AGENT WILBURN

Atlantastan

Chaos had erupted to a high degree since the clashing of the state and the criminals within the bounds of this wretched city. Members of the Wolf Gang were committing the ultimate violence in retaliation for Rude Boy's assault. The beef between the rivals of the Kiss Squad had communities and families terrified to step foot out of their homes. I had over three officers die on my watch since the beginning of this investigation a few months back, and I wanted justice for all the unlawful blood that was spilled. I wasn't stopping until every bullet in my clip and chamber found a home in the head of these hooligans. Then, I would reload the clip and empty it again.

Arriving at the federal facility in District 1, I stepped out of my car, ensuring that I was prepared for this encounter with the snakes in our backyard. The senator of the state had so much power and control inside the trenches because his word controlled every action in motion. He was dangerous on both sides of the field – a man in politics with an impeccable background for being the mastermind of this organization. He came from an elite bloodline, but it was only another fact that I didn't give two shits about.

Once I reached the third floor, I found the meeting room where the chief of the Federal Bureau and I were set to meet. I wanted more than just answers now. I wanted results, and I meant quickly.

Walking inside, his eyes met mine, and my expression said it all.

"Wilburn, before you go off the handle, I had no knowledge of this girl being undercover while my field was on. I mean, think about it. It was my ass that would've been on the line," he tried to explain.

"Chief, I'm gonna be very brief, and I won't sugarcoat a thing here today. You're starting to become suspicious to me, and that won't be good for you, sir. One of my agents is dead because of this nasty cult that you have lingering around this state, and it's all being done without consequence on your watch and under your supposed control," I said, making the quote-unquote hand gesture. "What makes you think that I don't know these people sleep in your backyard?"

He looked at me with an angry expression, as if my statement were an insult, and it should have felt like one. Not one time in my entire life had I seen a man of law enforcement allow so many lowlifes and thugs to overstep him in his position to defend the state. If he wasn't guilty, he sure as hell appeared to be. If you asked me, he was one of the main ringleaders.

"Listen, Agent Wilburn, let's not get ahead of ourselves and start placing inaccurate accusations on people. I've placed myself in the line of fire with every operation in this city. Now, these damn hooligans have terrorized local and government residents for at least six years around here, and the CIA hasn't stepped in not one goddamn time. Now, what I can tell you is that a full-blown war is about to break out around this zone, and you coming in to shuffle shit up is about to get everybody killed!"

"Chief, it seems that everyone around here has been dying long before anyone has been informed about any activity in your state. We all have a job to do. If that means a few more people have to die to get some understanding around here, then so be it."

"These crooks aren't the average, Wilburn. What aren't you getting through your thick skull? They're in every pocket, on every corner, within any organization. We have to be calm approaching these assholes, or we fold it all."

"You have an agent on the loose that is responsible for two of mine losing their lives, and that woman is gonna hang from a prison cell for eternity. You might be right across from her if the wrong scent of anything comes across my nostrils, Chief. That's a promise I can keep for sure," I warned him before turning to leave.

This city was going down piece by piece, and I was gonna be the guy standing tall through it all.

～

Rude Boy
Unknown District

The sharp jolt of pain that tore through my chest made me sit upright in a panic, gasping for breath, as my heart raced uncontrollably. My skin was drenched in sweat, sticking uncomfortably to the thin hospital gown I hadn't even realized I was wearing. It took a moment before my blurred vision cleared enough to take in the sterile, unfamiliar surroundings – a small, dimly lit room with stark white walls and cold tile floors. The air was thick with the sharp, metallic scent of disinfectant mixed with a faint medicinal tang. The steady, rhythmic beeping of a heart monitor filled the silence, competing with the dull hum of fluorescent lights overhead.

I pressed a trembling hand to the side of my head as a throbbing ache pulsed relentlessly behind my temples, as though each beat of pain struck in time with the monitor's rhythmic tone. The sudden creak of hinges sent a jolt through my already frazzled nerves, and my eyes darted toward the metal door slowly opening across the room. Someone was coming in, a shadowy figure stepping forward, silhouetted by the harsh fluorescent lighting of the hallway outside. Was this a nurse? A doctor? Or something entirely unexpected? My breath caught as I waited for them to step fully into view, every nerve in my body wound tight like a coiled spring.

Agent Porter quickly rushed over to me, grabbing my hand.

"Oh, my God. Rude Boy, are you okay?" she asked with concern.

I released a heavy sigh of relief. "I don't fucking feel like it. What the fuck is going on, and how long have I been here?"

"Rude, Taki shot you. You almost didn't make it. Bringing you back, it took everything we had. I even donated my own blood to keep you alive," Jamiyah said, her voice tight with exhaustion and frustration. "After you went down, everything spiraled out of control. Taki didn't just stop there. She took over the entire city. Atlanta fell completely under her grasp. It's been chaos since that day."

Her words hit me like a freight train, but shock turned quickly into urgency. I sat up straight, looking her dead in the eyes.

"Jamiyah… how long have I been out?"

"Two months," she answered firmly, though there was an edge of sadness in her tone. "You were in a coma, Rude Boy."

Two months. Two goddamn months. The weight of those words was suffocating. My mind raced with questions I wasn't prepared to ask. I hadn't heard from Shanti. No word from my crew. And now, this lunatic had the entire city wrapped around her finger. Everything we'd tried to protect had crumbled in my absence. I felt like I'd woken up in a nightmare I couldn't escape.

I clenched my fists, forcing myself to push through the panic. There was still a fight ahead, and I didn't have time to sit around dwelling on all we'd lost.

"We need to move." My voice came out sharper than I intended. "I need to get Shanti on the phone – right now. She needs to know I'm alive. And we are not leaving this city until Taki's body is spread across the Atlantic. My team needs to regroup. Now."

Jamiyah hesitated. I could see it in her eyes; she was torn between following orders and protecting me. It didn't matter. I wasn't about to stay in this hospital bed while our people suffered outside.

Moving sluggishly, Agent Porter retrieved her cell phone from her pocket. Something about her demeanor felt off, but I didn't have time to question it. She sifted through her phone and finally handed it to me.

"Look," she said quietly.

I glanced down, and my blood instantly ran cold.

Taki's face filled the screen, her smug expression twisted into something venomous and cruel. But it wasn't just her. It was Shanti and her father and mother. Strapped into restraints, each one of them were bound like prisoners waiting for the inevitable.

My heart pounded against my ribs, the heat of fury boiling through my veins. Whatever restraint I'd been clinging to shattered completely in that moment.

Taki's voice echoed through the video. She spoke with a mocking calmness that only fueled my rage further.

"Rude Boy," she began, her tone dripping with fake affection that made my skin crawl. "My love, my friend. I don't think you understand how serious this little dance between us really is. You thought some foreign army could save your precious bloodline? You underestimated me."

Her smirk widened as she waved a gun leisurely in the air, her arrogance burning through every syllable.

"You put your faith in the Nigerian Army, didn't you? But here's the problem. It's a failing system, run by men who'll turn into snakes for crumbs. They sold you – and your family – out without hesitation. And now, here we are."

Taki paused for dramatic effect, letting the weight of her words settle. Then came the punchline that sent my stomach into freefall.

"This is my warning," she hissed, her voice laced with venom. "You and your little crew will fall back, or I'll wipe out your entire bloodline, leaving nothing but ashes. You know I don't bluff."

Her gaze shifted to Shanti's mother, who whimpered helplessly. Taki raised her gun, the nozzle aimed squarely at her temple.

"And when you find this message, just know all bets are off. The next time I'm violated in any way..." She smirked darkly and tilted her head before delivering her final blow. "You can expect another one to fall. Just like this."

Without a second thought, she pulled the trigger.

Poc!

The video ended, but the image remained burned into my mind.

I never thought I'd witness what I just did, but the moment she pulled the trigger, I immediately placed the phone face down on the hospital bed, unable to look at it any longer. My chest tightened, and my thoughts raced as the weight of everything crashed down on me.

"How is this even possible?" I muttered, more to myself than anyone else. "This girl is tearing me apart piece by piece... I'm losing my whole damn family behind this bullshit."

I felt like the pit of hell had opened inside of me. My rage was volcanic, consuming every sane thought I had left. There was no talking this out. No reasoning. Taki had pushed too far, and every restraint I'd once held back was gone.

"Jamiyah," I growled, my voice low and deadly, "get the team ready. We're moving now. Taki's reign ends here. I'm burning everything she touches to the ground."

A close voice brought me back to the present. "Rude Boy, this isn't just any woman. This woman is different," Agent Porter said, sounding exhausted but brutally honest. "She's targeting you relentlessly. I don't think she'll stop until you two are either together or until one of you is dead. No matter what resources I try pulling together, this mess keeps growing because of her position. You need serious help – bigger help than what I can offer."

I sighed heavily and glanced around the room. "Where the hell is everybody?" I asked, my voice full of frustration and desperation, as I tried to figure out my next move.

Almost on cue, Ghost walked into the room, flanked by a few associates. The tension in the room shifted slightly with their presence, not easing but feeling a bit more grounded. Ghost grinned, giving me a firm handshake.

"Damn, look who finally woke up," he joked, masking concern with casual bravado. "Glad to see you pulling through."

I leaned forward on the hospital bed, rubbing my face with both hands, trying to clear the blur in my mind. Everything felt like a twisted labyrinth, and every turn led me closer to chaos.

"I appreciate you coming through, bro," I said finally. "But trying to prevail through all this feels like trying to climb out of hell with my bare hands." I paused, my voice tightening. "I've lost everything – the people closest to me, my stability, all of it. We might as well blow up the entire city so everyone loses. Those district leaders in Atlanta may fear Taki, but it's not because of how dangerous she is. It's because the bitch never stops when it comes to handling business. She keeps coming – relentless."

The bitterness in my voice lingered, but I kept going, choking back my frustration. "She's no ordinary player. She was Lo's righthand, his damn secretary, and the only way out of this mess is to expose her for what she really is. These district leaders need to see she's not untouchable. She's not God."

Ghost scratched his beard thoughtfully, his face hardening. "Look, I get all that, but right now, I can't tell she's anything less than unstoppable. She's got the press wrapped around her finger, and she's locked in tight with the cops – not just the street-level ones but the higher-ups. And don't get me started on the senator. She's tied to everyone who matters in this city."

He folded his arms across his chest, giving a slight shrug before laying out his plan without hesitation. "So, why don't we flip the script? Let's go after the ones protecting her – the dirty cops, the politicians, the people enabling her. We hit them where it hurts, bring chaos to their front steps, until she has nowhere to hide. That'll flush her out. Atlanta is only so big, and if she's really built like that, we confront it head-on. If the whole thing breaks in the process, so be it. We bring the fight to her – and everyone else – and let the streets decide who leaves standing."

Ghost's words hung in the air. They were cold and calculated, exactly what I expected from him, yet still unsettling. As much as I hated to admit it, he might be right. Atlanta was only so big… and if chaos was my new ally, maybe there was a way to turn this nightmare into something survivable. But even in that fleeting thought, I knew one truth. If we were going to do this, there would be no going back. And everyone might truly die before this ended.

"She's not going to let us get one over on her," I said, my voice thick with urgency. "I have to find a way to rescue my wife and her family before this girl completely erases my life. One wrong move and they could be dead. Who knows, she might have already pulled something foul behind the scenes." I detailed our precarious situation to ensure we didn't rush into any reckless decisions.

Agent Porter settled beside me, her expression a mix of solidarity and focus. "Listen to me," she began, her voice steady and reassuring. "Shanti and the rest of your family will be safe, and we will bring them back, but we have to finish this first. Taki won't risk hurting what you love, as that would strip her of her leverage. That's precisely why she keeps targeting your girl; she knows that's your Achilles' heel. Now is the time for us to strategize our next move. If we don't act wisely, we might not be able to recover from this."

I took in her words, aware she was right. The gravity of our situation pressed heavily on me. If I didn't get my family back, what was the point of going on? I would be consumed by vengeance, spending my days hunting down anyone who forced me to relive that unbearable memory.

"Tomorrow, we need to hit a few spots in some districts. There are people out there who still owe me favors, and I need to collect on them as soon as possible," I said, glancing over to Agent Porter for her input.

She folded her arms in a determined manner, a resolute look on her face. "Whatever it takes," she affirmed, echoing the intensity of my own resolve.

A silence settled between us, charged with purpose. I felt the weight of our mission pressing down on both of us, urging us to act before the darkness could entrap us any further. We needed to be clever and strategic, drawing from every resource we had, leaving no stone unturned in our pursuit of safety and salvation. In this battle, every moment counted, and I wasn't prepared to lose anyone else.

VINCE

It was eight in the morning when my car crept into the senator's secluded commercial lot. The sky hung low and burdened with heavy, grey clouds, casting a threatening haze over the city like a warning no one wanted to heed. A damp chill lingered in the air, and even though the streets were alive with movement, the chaos felt muted, like the city itself was holding its breath. This was no ordinary morning. It was the kind of gloomy, uninviting start that mirrored the tensions gripped tightly around Atlanta.

Inside the senator's world, something bigger was always happening. Every week, without fail, he met with the district leaders like clockwork. These meetings weren't just ceremonial. They were war councils, a chance for the powers that ruled with money and influence to regroup and reinforce their control. But lately, there was a shadow looming over the city, silently stretching its grip in a way that made even the most confident players keep glance over their shoulders. This "Rude Boy" character, whoever he was, had made his presence known without lifting a finger in public, and the pressure was squeezing the city like a vice. One thing about pressure though – it interrupted the flow of money. And that wasn't happening. Not on my watch.

I had made my name in these streets, clawing my way up to earn every bit of respect as Taki's lead enforcer and security chief. The rise in power had shifted everything for me – and for my people. Our reach extended far and wide, moving thirty kilos of meth along the south and east coasts just in the last two months. Success didn't just come from raw fear; it came from flawless execution. I had built connections with anyone willing to spend a dollar with the Kiss Squad organization, from big players to desperate underdogs hoping to survive. People didn't mess with us – not just because of what we might do but because of what we *could* do. Fear wasn't our only weapon; control over territory was just as deadly.

We were capitalists in Georgia, and we played the game ruthlessly. When the senator handed Taki full control over Atlanta, she proved herself quickly by shifting that control into power that no one dared challenge. It wasn't just her authority; it was the fear she carried with her like armor, a fear that allowed us to move freely and dominate every district, except for the "fuck-ass" authorities. They prowled like wolves – circling, sniffing for an opening, trying to disrupt the flow. But no one was putting us on the back foot. Not the Feds, not the cops, and certainly not this Rude Boy.

As I stepped out of my car, I couldn't help but glance through the dim light struggling to penetrate the clouds. The senator's lot felt isolated even in the heart of the city, surrounded by crumbling businesses and pockets of emptiness that somehow felt alive with tension. The air smelled damp, heavy, like it had absorbed the weight of conflict. The morning wasn't just grey; it was the kind of grey that seeped into your bones, reminding you that danger wasn't an abstract thought. It was real. It was coming. And as the city grew colder in its silence, I reminded myself of one thing: control wasn't given. It was taken. And we weren't letting go anytime soon.

I stepped into the building with purpose, heading straight to the elevator that would take me to the top floor of the senator's establishment. The echoes of my footsteps were muffled by the heavy carpet, but the weight of my presence wasn't lost on the staff who glanced my way and quickly avoided eye contact. On the top floor, I barely had a moment to adjust to the change in atmosphere before the senator's two security guards, straight-laced and radiating arrogance, stepped forward. Without a word, they gestured for me to follow them. Their silent demeanor spoke volumes about their attitude – a pair of glorified hall monitors who thought intimidation was a skill. They led me to a narrow stairwell that climbed up to the roof where the senator awaited me, perched comfortably in the lap of power.

On the rooftop, the greyness of the sky stretched as far as I could see, a fitting backdrop for the man who had positioned himself above it all. Sitting inside an all-black Blackhawk military helicopter, its intimidating silhouette blending perfectly with the dreary skyline, the senator and a handful of associates exuded authority. The rotor blades trembled slightly as the craft remained idle, a menacing reminder of its potential. I walked across the rooftop toward him, offering a slight nod, before climbing in and clasping his hand firmly in a handshake. His body-guards climbed in behind me.

"Senator, this is beautiful," I said, gesturing to the heights around us. "Now I see why you spend so much time up here, on top floors like this. You get to look down on everyone beneath you. That kind of power is intoxicating. We all crave it – dominance."

The senator, his expression calm yet sharp, met my gaze directly. "Power is knowledge, and knowledge is power, Vince. It's one and the same. Before becoming president – and I *will* become president – I vowed as a senator that I'd never loosen my grip when it came to the progression and rise of *my* people. My family is royal – and so are many other names in Georgia. It's my duty to ensure the avenues that keep us powerful remain open, no matter what happens. And that includes dealing with threats to that power."

He paused for a moment, letting the weight of his words sink in, before continuing. "We both know the Kiss Squad's been front and center at the FBI's radar since last year. They've been circling, watching. The heat you've drawn has made a few people… nervous."

He turned his attention to one of the men seated across from him in the helicopter. The man was an associate, but his posture sagged with unease, like he knew his leash was shorter than he realized. The senator motioned toward him with a smooth, almost casual gesture. "It's funny how threats often come from within. We had some chatter about a rat inside, someone feeding breadcrumbs to the Feds. We found him, Vince. Can you believe that?" He chuckled softly, though there was nothing humorous about the situation. "Let's take a little round trip. You need to see this."

Without waiting for an answer, the senator commanded his pilot to crank the engine, and before I could process it fully, the rotors were moving, and the heavy beast lifted into the air. The city beneath us seemed smaller by the second, its grey tones blurring as the helicopter ascended higher. The senator leaned back in his seat, his eyes drifting out the window to the endless sprawl below, as though he could see every moving part of the machine he had built.

"See, Vince," he said, his voice steady over the growing hum of the engine, "what I've learned in this life is simple. If you want to make an example, you need to do it publicly – make it loud enough that *everyone* sees it. Even the ones who think the lesson has nothing to do with them. The strongest move is always made by the man who's ready to risk it all to get what he wants."

As he spoke, I noticed one of his guards shifting in his seat. His movements were deliberate, calculated. A familiar tension hung in the air, and before I could fully register what was happening, the guard lunged forward. In one swift motion, he locked his arms around the neck of the man seated across from the senator. The man flailed briefly, panic taking over, but the second guard quickly moved in, securing handcuffs around his wrists, before forcing him to look directly into the senator's eyes.

The senator remained calm, unmoved by the chaos unfolding so close to him. There was no anger in his expression – just an eerie serenity that made the scene even more unsettling. The man tried to struggle, but his resistance was cut short when one of the guards drove a blade into his gut. A gasp escaped his lips, the sound sharp and desperate, but no one aboard seemed fazed. Blood began soaking his shirt as his body convulsed slightly.

I jerked forward in my seat, instinctively staring harder at the senator. "Hey, man — the hell's this supposed to be?!"

The senator didn't so much as flinch. His focus remained fixed on the window, his gaze passively moving over the city like he couldn't be bothered to respond. When he finally spoke, his voice carried the same controlled calm it always did, but there was an edge of satisfaction behind it – as subtle as the blade now buried in the gut of a man who clearly wasn't going to survive.

"Vince, I told you before… You're the future of this city." The senator's voice was calm yet firm, his tone carrying the weight of authority that could make or destroy careers with a single word. "I respect Taki and everything she's accomplished. The woman built one of the most ruthless crews Georgia has ever seen, and for that, she'll always have my admiration. But at the end of the day, this is a man's world – a world a man will *always* control. No matter how much power falls into other hands, there's only one kind of hand that can hold the reins fully… And you know that as well as I do."

He shifted in his seat slightly, glancing briefly at the bloodied man slumped forward in cuffs, his breath shaky and shallow. "My informant here, this piece of filth, has cost us millions over the last few months. His betrayal didn't just hurt our pockets; it burned our reputation. Atlanta is now the hottest city in the country for government scrutiny. The FBI, CIA, Homeland Security – you name it. The bastards are crawling all over it, combing through every crevice like rats in a dark alley." His jaw tightened, though his expression remained almost unnervingly calm. "And me? I'm the one sitting in the hot seat. All thanks to *him*. So you want to know why this is happening?" He gestured sharply toward the man with his chin. "This is how I deal with people who jeopardize my power, my *money*. Sometimes, you don't just send a message. You make it a lesson."

With a single nod to his guard, the senator gave his silent command. One swift motion later, the helicopter door slid open, the rushing wind roaring through the cabin like a broken dam. The guard holding the man didn't hesitate; he drove a hard kick into the man's back, sending him tumbling out of the chopper headfirst into the void below. The man's scream pierced the air as his body disappeared, swallowed by the grey horizon and lost to gravity's cruel pull. The muffled echo of it, drowned out by the spinning blades of the rotor, lingered like a ghost somewhere in the back of my mind.

I sat there, frozen for a moment, unsure of how to respond. Whatever statement the senator was making, loud enough for me to hear it over the chaotic backdrop, had my attention. Whether I was impressed, unsettled, or something else entirely – I couldn't tell. My gut churned, but my face didn't let it show.

The senator took a deep breath, like he was clearing his mind after a chore, and turned back toward me. "I'm sorry you had to see so much, but sometimes, business can't wait – even on days off. Work doesn't stop, not in this world." He sat back in his seat, the tension in his body easing slightly, though his presence remained just as dominating. "I'll keep this brief; I don't enjoy being in the air too long. This is just the only place where prying eyes and ears can't reach us. Now listen closely."

I nodded, leaning forward slightly. "I'm listening."

"My city, Vince." His voice dropped lower, carrying a sharp edge of frustration. "My city is being tarnished, depleted, gutted like a fish at the hands of reckless leaders who don't know how to keep their house clean. And I've lost more than I can tolerate because of it. Blood – blood that shouldn't have been spilled – is staining *my* streets, Vince." He leaned closer to me, his sharp eyes locking onto mine. "But that's not the worst of it."

My jaw tightened slightly, waiting for what he had to say next.

"My son, JoJo," he continued, his tone shifting to something darker, heavy with desperation masked by stoic control, "was taken. Kidnapped. And so far, the only thing I've received in return for my efforts to get him back is CIA heat and bloodshed – blood that came from *my* people. My followers. The ones I trusted." He shook his head, anger simmering beneath the surface. "Taki was sent on a mission to bring him back. No matter the cost, no matter the method, but she hasn't delivered. I promised her the reward of this city if she succeeded. That was supposed to be her crown. Instead, I've gotten nothing but bodies and chaos. And Vince... I can't lose another son. I've already buried one. If I lose JoJo, there'll be no coming back for me."

The senator held up his hands, palms open like he was presenting me with an offer on a silver platter. "I was thinking... you. You can help Taki, assist her, even take over if need be. I need JoJo back, and I need it immediately. You have the brains. The grit. The power to get it done. Do this for me – and the reward will be far beyond anything your imagination could dream of." He leaned back slightly, giving me just enough space to let everything he'd said sink in like a hook baited with both danger and promise.

I didn't need him to clarify. The senator wasn't just throwing words around to impress me; this was a challenge – one that carried the weight of life and death, not just for him but for me, for Taki, and likely for the crew we had built together. The question in the room wasn't if I would rise to it. It was whether I dared not to.

"You've got the right man for the job," I said, shaking his hand firmly before turning to look out the helicopter window.

I knew I wouldn't end up like my buddy who went headfirst into trouble. If tracking down this guy meant earning more respect and solidifying my position, I was ready to move forward. This was my opportunity, and I wasn't about to waste it. The meeting with this man went smoothly, and I'd make sure to let Taki know that when I spoke to her.

Soon, I wouldn't just be taking orders. I'd be making moves for the table.

〜

Taki
District 1

"I pulled a few strings outside of my crew and got this situation under control. You, on the other hand, sent your bumbling lackeys to interfere in Kiss Squad business – something you had no business involving yourself in from the start. Don't forget it's your son who is the root of all this chaos. We're supposed to be businesspeople, but lately, all it seems we do is kill for hire, and trust me, that is not part of my agenda." I leaned forward, my voice sharp and deliberate, as I made my point crystal clear to this sorry excuse of a senator for what felt like the tenth time.

My mind was on my revenge – a singular, all-encompassing focus. Taking down Rude Boy's pitiful little family and stashing them out of sight had shifted the balance of power squarely back in my favor. I was primed to stay ahead in this war, and I wouldn't hesitate to exploit every tool and opportunity to make sure I did.

The senator wasn't having it though. "Taki," he said, glaring at me as if his words carried the weight of a threat. "I don't think you understand the role you play in this game. But let me make one thing clear. I don't play by your rules. My youngest son is still missing, and for the record, the control of this city is still mine." His tone was laced with barely contained fury, but I couldn't help noticing how desperate he sounded beneath the bravado.

The tension crackled in the air like a live wire, but I remained unflinching. This wasn't a conversation anymore. It was a battle of wills, and I intended to walk away victorious.

"No, this city belongs to the district leaders who flush the currency through this city, and that's the reason I have arranged this meeting at the Club Cheetah tonight for this purpose. You want your position respected. You'll have the chance to confront every leader and decide who is with or against you on your own. The message is clear. You don't show. It's a sign of treason and will be handled accordingly."

"And what makes you so sure of this? We've been at it for months, trying to kill this one man and a team that seems to be unstoppable to you. Or is it maybe time to give every man a choice that leads to their success or demise? A few phone calls for desperate measures are rarely made but will be if necessary. I feel that you can bring this to a close. I need my last son. Whatever the cost. That said, however this plays out is on you." He leaned back in his chair with a blank expression.

His wife stood at his side quietly, waiting for my answer, and as always, I was prepared to have a plan in motion for the time when it was needed. It was all for what I wanted, and it was never any fun when the rabbit had the gun. I couldn't possibly rid this city of the Wolf Gang unless I gained complete control of this city, and in the next twenty-four hours, I planned to do just that.

～

Agent Jamiyah Porter

20

After returning to my safe house in District 6, I realized the fridge was a lost cause. Everything inside had spoiled. Fortunately, there was a store just across the street. With a few quick purchases, I managed to throw together a decent meal for the guys. They appreciated it, though the air was heavy with the weight of what was happening beyond our four walls.

Rude Boy had finally reunited with JoJo and a growing group of his soldiers. His numbers had swelled impressively, but the challenges ahead loomed larger than ever. The city was in chaos — a brutal fight for survival. Kiss Squad controlled almost every inch of Atlanta, leaving the rebellious districts clinging to life on the fringes. Rude Boy was holding the line of defense, barely keeping District 7 together.

It wasn't just the overwhelming power of the Kiss Squad causing trouble though. Taki was a wildcard in an already impossible situation. She wasn't just adept with strategies; she was ruthless and efficient. In a matter of weeks, she had carved out her own fiefdom in District 7, taking over key areas that once belonged to Rude Boy's allies. The Cubans' nightclub now answered to her, as did Ellery's diner. Even so, it wasn't clear if her intentions were aligned with the Kiss Squad's total control or if she had her own agenda.

District 7 had become a battleground, and Rude Boy had no choice but to continue the fight. Every move he made was crucial; the stakes were high. Taki's menacing presence lingered over him like a shadow, a constant reminder that survival in this city required more than just brute strength. It demanded careful strategy and maybe even a bit of luck.

Meanwhile, in District 1, she held dominion, shielded by the influence of the senator. Her grip on power was tight, and a single misstep could spell disaster for them all. The air was thick with tension as they gathered, faces taut with authority and fear. Their backs were against the wall, and if they didn't devise a plan quickly, the consequences could be fatal. Survival in this treacherous game was not guaranteed, and the urgency to outmaneuver their adversaries weighed heavily on them. Time was running out, and the time to act was at hand.

"Today marks your first day back, Rude Boy, and I know there's a lot on your mind. Our primary mission is to get your family back, but I fear the window of opportunity is closing fast," Ghost said, his voice steady yet filled with urgency.

"I couldn't agree more. I'm not going to waste any more time," Rude Boy replied, determination hardening his tone. "Ghost has promised to deploy his men to help us identify the most advantageous position for this fight. I can't afford to risk Shanti and her dad getting hurt. They've already lost her mom, and if anyone else gets caught in the crossfire, I swear I'll go all out to take this woman down."

"That's completely understandable. However, we need a solid plan," Ghost countered, his expression serious. "While we have some men at our disposal, I'm not convinced it's enough. The Feds have intensified their presence at night, making their operations increasingly ruthless. Their strategy is to eliminate threats before considering identification. We can't treat these cops any differently. If we're moving through the city to find this bitch, we gotta stand on business until this mission is complete. The weight of this situation is really starting to wear on me."

Ghost's honesty hung in the air, punctuating the gravity of their situation. Both men knew that they were navigating a treacherous path, and every decision would carry significant consequences. The tension between them was heavy, but beneath it lay a mutual understanding of their commitment to protect those they cared about. Time was of the essence, and they needed to act swiftly and decisively.

Rude Boy's voice carried the weight of his frustration as he spoke, his thoughts pouring out like a dam that had finally burst. "I know exactly how everyone feels right now. The truth is, I've already made the mistake of losing Shanti.– again. I've put more lives in danger and have been forced to relive the same nightmare twice. Now, I'm staring down a decision that could very well be my last. If we're going to have a chance, I need to convince a few of the more rebellious leaders to join our cause, even if it means swallowing our pride. Their help is crucial, no matter how much bad blood exists between us. Working together is the only shot we have to slow this bitch down."

Ghost listened carefully before cutting in. "And what leaders, exactly, do you think could be persuaded to come on board?"

"I know what you're thinking," Rude Boy replied with a weary sigh. "A lot of these dudes probably don't want anything to do with us, and I get it. We've been at odds with them for years. But at this point, it's like flippin' a coin. We either make the right call, or we'll all end up in a fight we can't win. I refuse to give the wrong answer here because if I do, only one side will make it out alive. Here's the plan: tonight, we head out and make propositions to every leader who might give us even a sliver of hope. We do the same thing tomorrow, hitting every corner of this city if we have to. After that, it won't matter if this bitch has an army or the goddamn National Guard backing her. Once we get enough people on our side, she won't be able to make a single move without facing resistance every step of the way."

The determination in his voice was sharp, cutting through the tension between the two men. Rude Boy's plan wasn't flawless, but it was clear he was prepared to do whatever it took to tip the scales in their favor. He had no choice but to turn enemies into allies, unite the fragmented pieces of the city, and ignite a wave of confrontation that could cripple Taki's grip on power. The stakes were rising, and the clock was ticking.

"You're right. This is something we all need to be on top of," I said, my voice steady. "That new kid – Vince. The one Taki put in charge of her street team? He's trouble, no doubt about it. A real loose cannon. He's young, reckless, and already acting like Atlanta belongs to him. He's dangerous, and so are the wild thugs he's got rolling with him. They don't just make noise; they bring chaos."

Ghost sat back, a frown shadowing his face. "And let's not forget," he said sharply, "we've got enemies crawling out of the shadows by the hour. Thanks to that bitch stirring everything up, we're fighting fires all over the place. So, the question is... who do we deal with first?"

I took a breath, weighing the options carefully before answering. "Districts 5 and 9," I said, leaning forward. "Anyone else? Right now, they're just gonna slow us down– a liability we can't afford."

Ghost raised an eyebrow and shot a glance at Rude, who stood nearby, listening intently. For a second, Ghost looked skeptical, like he didn't fully grasp where I was going with this.

"The Spanish and the Jamaicans?" Ghost asked cautiously, his tone low and deliberate.

"Exactly," I confirmed without hesitation.

Ghost snorted bitterly, leaning back in his chair. "Let me get this straight. You want to take the same crews we were just going toe-to-toe with – fighting in the streets – and convince them to fight with us now? To kill for us? You really think that's the play here?" He raised his hands as if to throw the whole idea back at me, clearly struggling with the shift in strategy.

I met his gaze firmly. "Yeah, that's exactly what I'm saying. It's risky, sure. But if we move right... they're the best shot we've got at balancing the scales."

Rude finally broke his silence, stepping into the light. "It's crazy," he said with a shrug, "but it's not stupid."

I could tell Ghost still wasn't all-in on the idea, but the way he frowned at the ground told me he was thinking – and thinking hard.

Rude Boy tilted his head, his silence speaking louder than words. The agreement was clear, unspoken but firm, like steel. We needed a solid plan, a way to carve a path through this mess, and Taki was the key. Without her connections reaching into the outside districts, she'd be forced to step out from the shadows and face us head-on. She might have been sharp, but even sharp edges had cracks.

What Taki didn't see, what her obsession with Rude Boy's down-fall blinded her to, was the vulnerability in her own armor. She left doors open – opportunities waiting to be exploited. And Rude Boy held a card no one else knew about but me, a hidden trump he'd been saving for the perfect moment. It was time to play it. Taki wasn't the only one who could sniff out weaknesses, and now, it was her turn to learn what happened when you overlooked your own.

～

Zeus

Upon arriving in Atlanta, I ensured a crew was ready for me and my team as soon as we crossed the city's borders. From the moment my foot touched the airport's pavement, I received comprehensive assistance for everything I'd need during my stay. Our accommodations – a luxury suite in District 3 – were already arranged, where we would reside alongside a few family associates. Italians didn't migrate heavily to Atlanta, making our presence here rare, and with that rarity came both challenges and privileges. When help was offered, I accepted graciously. However, no amount of preparation could brace me for the city's chaos. Within hours of settling in, I could already sense the need to clean up reckless behavior – behavior that, if left unchecked, could jeopardize our business interests.

Presentation was everything to me. A tailored two-piece Italian suit was my armor, a subtle yet potent message of strength and control. I lived by the belief that appearances were a reflection of power. But when my father's associate approached me for the first time, his opening remarks shattered any semblance of respect I might have afforded him. The man was bold, arrogant, almost insulting in his delivery.

"Your father sent you down here, huh? Well, you look barely over twenty-one, son. Just know, the people you're dealing with here are a handful. I hope you're not expecting everyone to make it out with you," he said.

Under any other circumstance, such an indirect jab would have ended poorly for him had one of my guards dragged him off a rooftop for his insolence. But I was here for a purpose – a family mission – and I wasn't going to waste energy on petty squabbles. The operation required focus, not frivolous distractions.

Our mission was clear: avenge my cousin Yazi's death. The pain of his loss ran deep, twisting every thought and sharpening my focus. My father's legacy demanded strength, and loyalty to family meant hunting down every answer, no matter the cost.

Early intelligence led me to one name—Rude Boy. He'd emerged at the edges of every rumor about Yazi's murder, a shadowy figure with uncertain motives. Men whispered about him, nervous and unsure, but I put no trust in gossip. Respect wasn't owed; it was proved. I judged men by the way they faced their own darkness, not by idle talk.

The first concrete lead I received was an address—Rude Boy's known hangout. That would be my next stop. Atlanta's glitter faded;

now, it was a city filled with ghosts and promises of violence. What had once been home was now hostile ground, where I'd bleed if I had to—but never lose.

Vengeance fueled every step. I needed answers about Yazi's killers. Rude Boy was the thread I'd follow until it led me to the truth. So I prepared to confront him, determined to deliver the justice our family deserved. If blood had to spill, so be it. The legacy my father built—and Yazi's memory—demanded nothing less.

AGENT JAMIYAH PORTER

After discussing what the next predicament would probably be for us, I assisted Rude Boy with loading up weapons and placing together passports and other sources of currency in case we had to abandon our mission and bail out. I felt like we had an understanding of what would happen if things went faulty, but for some reason, I could see Rude Boy's energy getting duller and tired. The frustration was written on his face, and the slight feelings that I was growing for him made it hard not to have some form of empathy. He wouldn't let this woman's blood be spilled for a lost cause, and it kind of showed me the reason this girl, Taki, wanted him for herself.

After gathering up the necessary shit for what we had ahead of us, we made our way out of my apartment and were met in the parking lot by a group of suited men armed with guns.

"And what the fuck do we owe this pleasure to?" Ghost snapped into action, aiming his gun with expertise.

Me, Rude Boy, and a few of his guards reacted on beat, and in a matter of seconds, guns were drawn. No one was speaking, and a trigger was bound to get pulled at any second. JoJo continued to look at Rude Boy as if he was waiting on permission to kill or be killed, but this was a thorn that we didn't need on our side right now.

"Who the fuck are you supposed to be? You damn sure ain't from round here looking like Walker the Texas ranger," Ghost asked with the gun still aimed at the man's head.

The armed men surrounding the man never spoke, but surely, they were ready to risk their lives from how firm they stood around him.

He smirked arrogantly before taking a few steps forward. I took a step closer myself.

"Please, we don't want any trouble. Just two groups of people that aren't trying to clash with each other. If you'll excuse us." I tried to kill the tension but was cut off by the well-dressed Black man in front of me.

"Speak for yourself when it comes down to clashing because my purpose of being here is standing right in front of me. I'm sure the name Yazi may refresh your memory a little, or have you tossed his innocent soul to the shadow realm like you do the rest of your flunkies?"

Hearing the name, Yazi, I watched Rude Boy's facial expression harden. It was not because of anger but more of regret and empathy. He slowly forced me to lower my gun and glared directly into the man's eyes before speaking.

"Yazi was family. Yazi was my friend, a loyal friend. Now, I'm not sure what you're insinuating here, but you can bet that I'm out here putting shit in the ground for that kid since I lost him."

"Well, let me properly introduce myself. You can call me Zeus Blackstar. I'm here on behalf of the Italians who wanna know why my cousin was murdered. Not only do I need answers, I need death to accompany me on my way back home. I was alerted to you back home. Heard to be one of the meanest guys inside the walls of this little city. But you're not too mean to allow my cousin's death without an answer for his family. You all have disrespected us to the utmost, but I'm only here for one reason. To handle the business with who's responsible. Now, either you're informing me on who I need to see or we're all dying right here, right now." Zeus spoke calmly to Rude Boy.

"Sounds like my kind of party," Ghost quickly chimed in.

Rude Boy held up his hand, signaling for him and JoJo to stand down. He stared in the eyes of the strange traveler, and I could see the form of respect he was gathering for what was just said.

"Maybe we need to step back inside and discuss a few more things like gentlemen. I can assure you that I'm not your enemy, but the person who is will surely accept all the smoke you have to offer," Rude Boy stressed before opening the door for the group of Italians to enter.

There was so much piled on top of our heads that this only made things a tad bit worse. Death was high in the atmosphere, and different sources of trouble were stepping from the shadows from secret affairs in business that Rude Boy just wasn't prepared for. My mind was already made up that I wasn't losing another person beside me, let alone allow this bitch to have the press on the entire town because she craved power and a nigga that didn't want her. Lying down was out of the question, but dying was damn sure the objective if this shit was necessary. We needed more than clarity. We needed this shit ended once and for all.

Vince

Linking up with the Kiss Squad had transformed my entire hustle, turning me into a powerhouse in every corner of the city. Our crew wasn't just the top earners in the south; we were the ones making untouchable players tremble at the sound of our name. Fear wasn't just a concept; it was a tangible force we carried wherever we moved. I spent most of my time posted at the escort house over in District 9, a spot owned by Taki herself. Taki wasn't your average hustler or leader; she was sharp, calculated, and unapologetically fierce. While others in the game tried and failed to establish a foothold in the escort business, she'd mastered it, building an empire from scratch. In a world dominated by men, she'd taken the crown and was running things with the same ruthless efficiency that earned Frank Lucas his place in history. Yet somehow, she had made it her own.

The operation was seamless. A few of my soldiers roamed around the house, spending money with the ladies, keeping things flowing. Escort business in District 9 wasn't just any secret business; it was a playground for power. Upstairs in the private VIP section, we offered anything a client could imagine. Privacy was guaranteed, and nothing was off-limits. Drugs? We had them. Food? We had that too, fresh and abundant. Merchandise ripe for hustling? Stacked in the back. And of course, there was no shortage of women available to cater to every need: white, Black, Asian, Brazilian, Albanian, you name it. This place wasn't just a business; it was the ultimate haven for indulgence. All anyone had to do was pick what they wanted, and the house delivered.

"Yo, Vince, there's a guest out front asking to halla at you," my youngest recruit said, pulling up to my side.

I gave him a deadpan look. "A guest? Nigga, every guest I invited here is already inside." Glancing at the time on my watch, I motioned for my steppers to follow me, alert but calm.

Navigating the luxurious hallway, I kept my eyes sharp as I made my way to the living room at the front of the house. The elegant space was dimly lit, but the tension in the air was brighter than any chandelier hanging overhead. When I stepped into the room and laid eyes on the group of men stationed in the middle of our business grounds, my instincts immediately kicked in. These weren't regular clients here for pleasure. They had an edge that felt heavy, almost stifling.

I strutted toward them, my guards shadowing my every step, scanning the men one by one as I approached. My voice was cool, unbothered. "Good evening, fellas. Anything I can do for y'all tonight? You all know we've got every flavor of a bitch you could ever dream of in this building, so don't hesitate to treat yourselves. It's all here for the taking," I said, letting a smile tease my lips, though my gut told me this wasn't an ordinary visit.

The man who stepped forward looked vaguely familiar, his face hovering somewhere in the fog of my memory, but I couldn't place him. He didn't waste time with pleasantries. "We ain't here for any bitches tonight. Word is you're the face behind that chick, Taki. We've got some unfinished business with her, and I happen to be very serious about finding her. Figured you'd be the right person to help."

As he spoke, my mind raced, piecing together the undertone of his words, the way his nerves seemed controlled but on the edge of snapping. These niggas weren't here for pleasure; they were here to press me. And pressing me about Taki? That was dangerous terrain for anyone to step on.

I glanced at my guards, giving them a silent signal that immediately raised the red flag. My instincts tightened, preparing me for what was coming next. And then it hit – a deafening boom.

The sound ripped through the room before I had time to react. One of my shooters crumpled to the ground like deadweight, his head blown clean off his shoulders. Blood splattered against the sleek walls, staining the polished perfection of the space.

The chaos was instant, but my head was already there. This wasn't a guest; this was war walking into my house. And now, it was time to handle it.

The next shot whizzed past my ear, nearly grazing me. Instinctively, I took off running, desperate to find cover as my boys traded fire with the ambushers. My heart pounded in my chest as I stumbled across the blood-slick floor, heading for the back exit. Gunfire erupted all around me, bullets flying like they were chasing us down in cold blood. These dudes weren't just coming for our heads. They were wiping us out like wild dogs.

"Boc! Boccc! Boc!" The sharp cracks of their weapons echoed through the building.

By the time I reached the hallway, adrenaline surged through me. I reached down to my ankle and pulled out the small nine I kept there for emergencies. There was no aiming – just survival. I fired at anything that moved in my line of sight.

"Poc! Poc! Poc! Poc! Poc! Poc!"

With the back exit finally in reach, I threw my shoulder into the door, but it didn't budge.

"Fuck!" I stepped back and kicked it open with a desperate force. I backed out of the exit, firing two shots into the chaos, until my gun clicked empty. Knowing it was useless now, I tossed the weapon aside and ran for my life. Getting caught in the crossfire wasn't an option – not today, not ever. No way could I let these fools take me down in our own place of business. Somewhere deep inside, rage burned like fire at the thought of the man who had the guts to pull this shit off – not just to come for us but to try and tear apart everything we'd built.

The events of the last few seconds blurred together as I cut through the pathway outside that led back around to the front entrance. Glancing over my shoulder, I caught sight of the men storming out of the building, their weapons at the ready. I hauled ass to the car, praying I'd make it out of this carnage — and not just me but my people too.

Sliding into the driver's seat, I kept one eye fixed on the chaos behind me. There were gunshots still ringing out when two of my boys – shirts streaked with blood and faces grim – flung open the doors and jumped inside. I barely had time to catch my breath before I saw D, my last man, sprinting for the car at full speed.

"Come on. COME ON!" I shouted, gripping the wheel so tightly my knuckles turned white. But D wasn't fast enough. The echoes of gunfire turned sharper, louder, and I saw him drop to the ground. My gut twisted as his body jerked violently, blood spraying from his head like a gruesome fountain, before he crumpled in a lifeless heap on the pavement.

"Shit!" The word ripped out of me, raw and angry, as I slammed the gas pedal to the floor. Tires screeched, hearts raced, and I didn't dare look back again. My mind kept replaying the image of D hitting the ground, his brains blown out in the blink of an eye, but I couldn't stop now. I couldn't let his death – or this blatant attack – go unanswered. They didn't just try me. They tried all of us. And eventually, I was going to take that bastard's head for daring to come at me like this.

Bullets slammed into the car, ricocheting off the doors and hood like angry sparks. I could hear metal pinging and glass cracking, and I kept my head ducked low beneath the dashboard, gripping the wheel with sweaty palms. As soon as I peeled out of the driveway, my lungs burned, struggling to keep up with my rapid breaths. Adrenaline still coursed through my veins, but the disbelief hit me hard. Our spot. They ran down on us in our spot. The rage was bubbling up faster than I could swallow it, and I knew deep in my gut that this wasn't random. This hit wasn't just about territory or money. It had *their fingerprints* all over it – the reckless way Taki and that senator were handling our moves lately. Slipping up, cutting corners, and running their mouths too much. Too many mistakes had piled up, and I should've snatched control a long time ago before it spiraled to this.

This was survival now. And anyone who didn't move with precision? Anyone who didn't follow my lead? They wouldn't be moving at all.

AGENT WILBURN

After getting to the infested city, I knew I had my hands full with snatching these criminals off the streets, but I was always prepared for a challenge. I had the names of all the big shot callers who had been making noise over the last four years, and those were the ones I was hunting down. Nothing was off limits, and there weren't any districts that my men weren't allowed to cross. I made my way down to Midtown in District 1 for a sit down addressing Chief Mason. He had a few things to vent about, and regardless of how much seniority he possessed in this state, we were still enforcers of the law against the ones overstepping and breaking it.

Getting down to the district attorney's office, I flashed my badge to alert the woman at the front desk that I had arrived. My key was to inform all government officials on the best way to tackle this city. I also wanted to let it be known that Chief Mason would no longer be in control of the operations taking place inside Atlanta. The power of the police had escaped his grasp, and it was sad to say that he wasn't capable of leading the wrongdoers to justice. In the past month, I'd had two agents murdered on his watch, and that slip up would go on no longer.

Entering the building, I signed in at the front desk, took the elevator up to the eighth floor, and got off. The lead advisor, Ms. Jones, was present at the front desk and waved me over just as she ended a phone call.

"Agent Wilburn, it's not even 9:30 yet, and you're jumping on a case log. I gathered all the information you requested. We have over five leads that can give us feedback on your request, and I've also gotten word that Agent Porter is the first suspect that we should be trying to reach our hands out and grab. After her partner, Lace, was murdered, her name has been stretched across the federal database. She knows too much, and I hear that she's also helping out the murderer."

"Murderer?" My brows rose.

"Khalifa Bah."

I nodded slowly taking in the information. "Yep, seems like she's helping his side out for some awkward reason. We have had over thirteen incidents since she went rogue. I don't know about you, but Chief Mason and everyone else don't seem to notice that we have a federal agent coaching criminals around our system." I released a heavy sigh in frustration. "For some reason, I'm quite sure that they have an idea. Not too many things can slip through Mason's hands and pass his eyes. He was trained to see what the average eye didn't. I'm confused about how he doesn't have an answer for any of this." I made my way toward the briefing.

As I made my way down the hallway, I reached the office and could hear Mason's voice before I stepped in. I stopped to listen for a second. Turning the knob, I walked in, and the room fell quiet. Mason and five other agents were gathered around the table in front of the projector screen. A few faces were under the device but none that I recognized from any cases I'd been involved with.

"Agent Wilburn, I thought that we were set to meet this Monday. Still a pleasure, of course. Is there something I can assist you with?"

I walked over, taking a seat next to him, before I glanced down at my watch. I knew that I didn't have time to waste, nor did I want to search and dig for lost information that I should have already been aware of. I was going to let it be known where the CIA enforcement stood.

"Yes, there is, Chief Mason. It's been brought to my attention that your job description is not being pushed to the best of your ability, and may I say that you were one of the best agents I've ever trained and worked with, so of course that statement is a shocker. Is there anything critical relating to this crackdown that I need to know about?" He gave me a curious eye as if I knew something that he didn't. I never exposed my hand when it came down to having the lead, so I paid attention instead of spilling what was already known.

"Uh, I don't think I can recall. I'm quite sufficient with this, so I would remember. I'm building a border around this whole sting operation, so we cover every base possible. You know just as much as I do." He shrugged before taking a seat.

"Well, maybe I'm just light years ahead of you all, or you guys are working with the enemies. I've been in this town for a few days, and I have the names of everyone who has caused the most crimes here in Atlanta, some of the biggest you can think of. If I know who they are, I'm quite sure that you are aware as well. I'm not positive on the dirty shit that's taking place outside of this government building, and I'm not too pressed in finding out. I just would like to know who's involved, so I can stop it. I want to be briefed on everyone that's booked, charged, or has information on my crew leaders, Taki and Rude Boy. Double up on security shifts, and no officer is to move around with less than four backup units. I want mouths closed and ears open. I've heard that these renegades don't mind killing cops or even crossing out their kind. I know exactly what we're dealing with, and yes, we must be careful, but the one thing we will not do is allow these killers to override the law. We make it, so let's enforce it."

I could see that Mason wasn't taking my comment too lightly, but that was exactly what I needed from him.

"What's that supposed to mean, Agent Wilburn? I mean, we've all been working hard at this for years to bring this threat down, and now you think after stepping in it for a few hours that you have everything figured out, which is absurd. Khalifa Bah is dangerous. Taki is a cold-blooded monster, and before anyone brands the idea of working with a criminal, they would be treated as such. I've had this job this long for a reason, sir." He folded his arms with an aggravated expression.

That was exactly what I needed to see, but I just moved smarter. I envisioned how all this would fall, and if I was correct, Chief Mason was going to fall directly into my hands. I couldn't see the full picture of where it all stood, but I surely could smell bullshit in the air.

"Just as I said, the CIA is here to take down every crew member, criminal, and criminal government official that hides in this state. I can assure you of that. I hope the criminals are the only ones that remain on that list. Inform your team that there is a mandatory check in of every search and takedown that is placed. I want to know everyone who's booked. It's time to start finding out exactly who we're dealing with in these districts."

I stood from my chair and left Chief Mason to drown in his thoughts. I knew that out of everything he took from me, he understood my warning about being onto him. I was about to break this city street by street. Once my authority was finished being placed into the area, I would run Atlanta.

⪘

Taki
District 1
Club Cheetah

Tonight was more than my night of celebration. It was an act of dominance, a call to my power and how far I was willing to go to prosper from what was rightfully mine. Word of Rude Boy finding his way back to the city after his near-death experience caught wind to my ear. I loved him, sure enough, but if the option of choosing Shanti over me stuck inside his brain, he would never sleep comfortably for the rest of his life until I drained all the blood from his body.

My new recruiter, Vince, was the lead of the Kiss Squad, while I was out attending to business around Atlanta. Fierce wasn't a word for him. He killed when necessary, and there was no understanding if it wasn't coming from our side. His dark skin and evil eyes forced people to veer from his lane, but whatever word I gave, you could ensure that it was completed.

I strolled back toward my section from the small office in the back after forwarding the wire transfer to my overseas account. My time was gonna be over inside this city soon, but my statement would remain forever.

"Yo, Taki, where you been, boss lady? Everyone is here for this meeting, but the Spanish bitch over District 5 now says she still has no business to discuss with you unless it's you and her to the death. What you wanna do?" Vince asked with enthusiasm.

"Patience. Things are so clear now, you can step over shit a mile away. We encourage our district leaders to keep loyalty or die without it. The government is in town, and it's likely the only reason people aren't getting blown away in front of the precincts, but even with the police, the gloves are easily coming off. Let's get this meeting out of the way." I stepped into my large VIP section and joined the table with the eight different district leaders who were willing to negotiate business or wage war if the pages didn't match up the same.

"Good evening to all of you lovely bosses. I'm glad you showed your respect and genuineness by attending my uh... shall I say summit?" I gazed around at all of them.

"Feelings are mutual. To be honest, I never had any intention of coming because the laws of what we portray to stand on aren't being fucking applied," Pekay spoke up for District 5, which was Mendez's old territory

I could sense tension on his chest, but he knew not to overstep too far.

"I can assure you all that you will be answered to as quickly as possible. This entire city has been in chaos, and everybody wants off the leash. Killing is necessary, especially when these rules get broken."

The senator cleared his throat, rudely interrupting me, before standing up.

"If I must say, we can all cut the small talk. It's quite simple that we're all here for a purpose. You district leaders have been occupying my city, polluting drugs in the air, extorting businesses, killing dedicated law officials, and a bunch of other shit that we can talk about for years, right? Those times don't matter anymore. Only now. I need my son back, and I'm willing to pay the price."

"Oh, yeah, and what price may that be?"

"Whatever a person can try in their wildest imagination. This is not a fucking nursery. We sell drugs in this city and murder the ones who are too weak to continue beside us. This Rude Boy has folded my life in the nastiest way imaginable, and I can't sit back and allow that to happen. So, I have a few people who will also be added to the phone. This is Clark and Joe. They're ex-military and probably the only ones that aren't scared to go headfirst at this job. The first to the finish line takes it all." He stared around the table at us all.

"Wait just one minute, Senator. Let's be sure to remember our manners now. I invited you here to be a part of this next step because you were so behind. Let's not forget that we have an agreement already on the table, and I can never be thrown to the curb for what I've implemented in this city. That would be so stupid and naïve of you," I warned, trying to hold onto the little composure I did have.

"And feeling that the life of my son isn't more important than your beef is a thought of an imbecile. Taki, you are a powerful source for this team, but your power will never be sufficient enough to override what I want and when I want it. You can consider this situation handled, and my assistants will finish the mess that was started. But I do thank you for all the support that's been given."

I stared at him as all of our guests sat quietly, waiting for me to speak. This was a stupid, old man indeed, but for sure, I was about to switch that pathetic mind frame of his to believe in me.

"Sure thing, Senator. I guess this meeting is adjourned. Let it be known that we're at liberty to engage in all opposition, and please grab this little kid, so this shit can end. Happy killing." I stood from my chair and signaled for Vince to follow me.

I moved through the reservation area, across Club Cheetah's dance floor, until I reached the other side. I had all eyes and ears on me, but that didn't matter.

"Wassup, Taki? Looks like you're ready to get on my type of time. What do I need to do first?" he asked me eagerly.

"Do what you do best, of course. Kill. I want Rude Boy alive. If you can handle this small assignment, I might think about giving you a chance with laying next to something as spectacular as me."

"Damn, it's like that? This beef with this nigga, Rude Boy, must be serious, huh?"

"That's for me to worry about and for you to handle. Just get it done if the shoe fits the foot," I responded before leaving out the front entrance.

AGENT WILBURN

District 13

Early the next morning, I overheard a critical piece of information: the location of the Kiss Squad leader. The city was drowning in chaos – a flood of lawlessness spread by ruthless crew members consumed by nothing but evil intent and the power to destroy. Their presence was a contamination, tearing apart the city I swore to protect. There was no room for hesitation. My plan was decisive: to get rid of their entire clan by any means necessary. Killing them all was the only path forward, and I was the man prepared to step into the fire to ensure its success.

With a ten-man SWAT team by my side, I launched a full-scale operation designed to dismantle this criminal empire. My orders were clear: find, arrest, and eliminate every last Kiss Squad and Wolf Gang crew member from the streets of Atlanta. It was time to get rid of them for good. The city deserved freedom from their grip, and I was determined to deliver it.

We fortified a four-block perimeter, anticipating potential escape attempts in case the plan spiraled into a chase. But failure wasn't an option on my watch; I would personally ensure these criminals didn't get a single chance to flee. Everything was mapped out to precision, and the resolve within me burned stronger than ever. It wasn't just about taking back the streets; it was about proving, once and for all, that justice wasn't something to fear; it was something to enforce. The fight for peace had begun.

"Lieutenant Washington, I need your men covering the backside of this house. Keep your eyes sharp. Nothing happens without my direct order. If anyone resists or makes a false move, you handle it. If they fight back, you take them out, along with anyone riding with them. Do you understand?"

"Yes, sir," Washington replied without hesitation, immediately springing into action as I directed.

Tensions were already high. The FBI's chief had been skating on thin ice, his leadership riddled with sloppy tactics that had left this operation hanging by a thread. If it took the CIA to crack the code on this secret criminal ring, so be it. Everything else would fall in line afterward. For now, I had no choice but to lead the charge myself and ensure every decision counted.

As we rolled into the narrow confines of the designated street, the weight of the operation pressed down on me. This wasn't just another bust; failure wasn't on the table. We unloaded from our vehicles, armed to the teeth and prepared to face whatever resistance stood in our way. Every movement, every sound around us, was amplified in my mind. It was the calm before the storm, and I could feel the chaos lingering just beneath the surface.

"Let's move in. Stay sharp and remember – one false move and we neutralize everything in range." With a sharp gesture, I signaled for my team to advance.

The first squad breached the black security gates, spreading out across the driveway with tactical precision. For a brief moment, there was only silence – the kind that filled the air before everything cracked wide open. And then it started. A stampede of gunfire erupted as bullets rained down from all directions.

The sudden sound of ricocheting slugs slammed against my SUV with a deafening fury, forcing me to duck instinctively. My truck rocked as shot after shot struck its frame, and then, in an instant, all hell broke loose.

Boom!

A loud, shattering blast cut through the chaos as my windshield exploded. I felt the heat of shattered glass before my driver let out a strangled gasp; a single bullet had gone clean through his skull. I watched in disbelieving horror as the side of his head ruptured open. Blood sprayed across the dashboard as his body slumped forward, lifeless, against the steering wheel.

I couldn't afford to stop and process the loss. The operation had shifted from an organized assault to pure survival. Chaos engulfed the street, and the only option left was to take control and fight our way through. Damn it, this was war.

"Move out! Let's go!" I shouted, kicking open the passenger door and leaping out with my rifle locked and ready. The chaos was already swallowing us whole. I had barely hit the pavement before spotting a Kiss Squad thug standing right in front of the house, and I didn't hesitate. I raised my rifle and pulled the trigger.

Boc! Boc! Boc!

Poc! Pok! Poc!Poc!

The first body hit the ground, but the turmoil was just beginning. My men hadn't even breached the threshold of the property when the armed criminals retaliated. From the sides of the house, they poured out like rats in a fire – shouting, guns blazing, bullets tearing through the air. Their firepower spoke louder than their voices, and just like that, the operation exploded into a bloody war zone. This wasn't just an arrest anymore. We were locked in a full-blown shootout at the Kiss Squad headquarters.

"Cover me!" I roared into my radio over the gunfire, adrenaline pounding in my veins. "Call for reinforcements! Get me four backup squads down here now!" My order was sharp and absolute. There wasn't time for half-measures; we needed all hands on deck if there was any hope of survival.

Ahead of me, another thug charged into view with his weapon raised, and I acted without hesitation, delivering a direct shot straight between his eyes. The man dropped instantly, crumpling to the ground in a lifeless heap.

Boom!

The sound of my gunfire was deafening, but the chaos around me was louder. Without a second to think, I pressed forward, unloading every bullet I had as I advanced toward the entrance to the property. The air was thick with the smell of gunpowder and hot metal as a barrage of shots rang out around me.

Boom! Boom! Boom! Boom! Boom!

It wasn't just a firefight; it was a battlefield. The thunderous exchange of gunfire, the cries of pain, the urgency of survival – it dragged me right back to the deserts of Iraq. The harsh reality hit me like a gut punch: war didn't care where you were. It didn't stop for cities, for neighborhoods, or for quiet homes lined with fences. It found its way into every corner. And as much as I hated it, I was reliving the horrors I'd once tried to leave behind – the split-second decisions between life and death, the shredding noise of bullets cutting through air and flesh.

My team moved like a hive of soldiers born for combat, scattering across the property with military precision, trading fire, shot for shot. Every move counted, every bullet mattered, every life was weighed in seconds. We were knocking down criminals one by one, paving the way through death and desperation.

I couldn't afford to think about the casualties or the cost — not my driver, not the lives lost here, not even my own. All that mattered was survival and the mission. We had started this war, and now, there was only one way to finish it – by leaving no man standing at the top.

"On your left!" I yelled, my voice sharp with urgency, as I spotted a killer emerging from the shadows beyond the doorframe, double-barreled shotgun in hand. The warning barely had time to register before the room exploded with the deafening thunder with a *Boommm!*

Time froze in a gut-wrenching instant as I saw the shotgun's slug punch through my lieutenant's Kevlar vest and bury itself deep into his chest. He staggered backward, his movements faltering as crimson blood began to seep through the tactical gear. My heart pounded in my ears like a war drum, every beat driving the chaos around us further into focus. The dimly-lit hallway was a maze of smoke, shadows, and adrenaline, and my lieutenant was down – clawing at life as he fell heavily against the wall. But there was no time to think, no room for hesitation.

With the gravity of the moment crashing down on us, my team surged forward, kicking into high gear like a force of nature. Tactical boots hit the ground hard as we charged toward the residence, a storm of urgency and determination. Somewhere in this labyrinth of opulence was the boss – the mastermind behind it all, waiting in the darkness like a predator. The house was a over-the-top display of excess; white marble floors gleamed beneath crystal chandeliers, and gold-trimmed furniture promised a life of luxury bought with blood money. But for all the glamor, the reality hung heavy in the air. Countless kilos of drugs were scattered across the tables, piled high in plain view – evidence so incriminating it practically screamed to be confiscated.

This wasn't just a raid; it was a battle for justice. Every ounce of adrenaline, every piece of evidence we secured here, wasn't just about taking down a violent criminal empire. It was about building a case that wouldn't crumble, a case that could finally turn the tides against this ruthless operation. Through the chaos and pain, the mission was clear: survive, persevere, and bring them down piece by piece.

"Clear the upstairs!" I barked, motioning for a team to sweep the top floor. Another group followed close on my heels as we moved through the hallways of the massive main floor. Every room had to be secured, every corner cleared. This was no time for half measures.

As I rounded a corner, my muscles tensed. My ears caught something – a sharp, sudden movement in the distance. Someone was trying to make a break for it. I eased forward, rifle at the ready, until I saw him – one of the Kiss Squad grunts bolting for the back door through the kitchen. He reached the burglar bar gate in desperation, only for his luck to end there. The locked bars forced him right into the path of my gun. I lunged forward, slamming the butt of my rifle into his chest and sending him crashing against the door.

"Don't even think about it," I growled, pressing the barrel of my gun against his head. "I'll kill you without hesitation. But before we get to that, you're gonna answer some questions. Now, tell me – where's your scumbag of a leader? Who's taking the blame for the death of my officers?"

His eyes widened in terror. "Please! Please don't kill me!" he stammered through trembling lips, clearly terrified beyond belief. "Y-You don't gotta do nothing! I swear! I don't even work under that boss. I'm just here to count the money. I swear to God; I'm only sixteen!"

Sixteen. That explained the fear on his face. But I wasn't giving him an easy way out. "Don't waste my time, kid. Where's the person in charge?" I pressed harder, gesturing toward the cuffs dangling from my belt. "What's the Kiss Squad planning? And before you give me excuses, listen closely – either you tell me where I can find the ringleader, or I make you take the initiative yourself."

Without waiting for his answer, I snapped a pair of cuffs onto his wrists. The cold steel rattled as I tightened them.

"No way in hell! Why would I make you work hard to find her when I can tell you everything? I'll give you the whole damn story, man!" His words spilled faster than I could process them, his voice trembling with desperation. "You want info? Fine. I'll give you what nobody else will – everything you haven't been told and everything they've been keeping hidden!" He shook his head, panic visibly overtaking him as he cracked under pressure.

I studied him closely. His street clothes were worn and cheap, his face scant of anything resembling confidence. He wasn't a powerful player – not even close. Just another kid caught in the mix of grownups' criminal mess. They'd left him behind in this chaotic den, tasked with counting money, while his crew ran wild in the streets. He wasn't important; he was expendable. A pawn, nothing more. And now he was scared enough to become the most valuable thing I had: a snitch. The kind of snitch that would ditch loyalty without thinking twice.

With him in cuffs, I wasn't getting just a minor criminal. I was getting an informant – a kid that knew exactly where to find the Kiss Squad leader, willing to talk fast and throw the wolves straight into the fire. That made him priceless. Whether he gave up the info out of fear or a desperate need to save his own skin didn't matter to me. Either way, this case had just taken a turn, and I planned to use it to my advantage.

～

Chief Mason

I had been under heavy fire for weeks now, dealing with the incident of chaos sparked by the arrest and the reckless hooligans still tearing through the city. Every superior seemed to have me squarely in their sights, fueled by Agent Wilburn's relentless insistence that he was onto something – a theory he refused to let go of. I respected Wilburn's intellect; he was sharp, no doubt. But when it came to navigating the murky waters of business and pulling strings without leaving a trace, I was leagues ahead of him. It had always been my forte: getting things done and walking away unscathed.

Tonight wasn't any different. I arrived at Taki's secluded estate, tucked neatly away on the outskirts of District 11. The air was thick with tension, the kind that demanded unwavering vigilance. Driving up the expansive driveway, I slowed to a stop before the towering gates, buzzing the intercom for entrance. A camera overhead shifted its focus, recording my every move. Moments later, a faint crackle through the microphone confirmed what I suspected. They were watching me.

When the gates slid open, I felt the familiar surge of adrenaline. My mind accelerated, running through every possible contingency. Meetings with someone like Taki were as unpredictable as they were crucial. While she'd made me an obscene amount of money since our partnership began, the stakes were always high. Her influence stretched across Atlanta like wildfire, unchecked but lucrative. Our agreement granted her free reign for expansion, provided I got my cut. That understanding had forced the senator – and every district leader, for that matter – into irrelevance. In my world, their power meant nothing. If I wanted, I could flip the script overnight. I held sway enough to trigger martial law, bringing the full force of the federal government crashing down on the city's renegades. But I had no interest in bloodshed – not when this business could be handled with discretion. Collateral damage was bad for profits, and innocent lives were too costly to expend.

Two of Taki's men greeted me at my car. They kept their distance, their body language reassuring me that no foolishness was coming my way. Still, I'd learned to never walk into any room without a backup plan. A quiet confidence followed my every step as they escorted me inside, leading me to the grand living room where Taki was perched on her sofa. She was as collected as ever, but the scene before me struck like a slap across the face.

Out of instinct, my gaze darted away as I caught sight of a man – his face buried between Taki's legs, tongue twirling around her clit. She was completely naked except for a pair of heels and a gold ankle bracelet. The audacity of the moment wasn't lost on me. But if there was one thing I had learned, it was not to let surprises unravel my composure. Any crack in my armor could leave me exposed, and meetings like this required me to stay sharp.

"Oh, my God, seriously? How are we supposed to have a conversation like this?" I asked one of Taki's guards as I tried to process the bizarre display unfolding right in front of me.

The guard shrugged indifferently, his expression devoid of sympathy. Clearly, I wasn't going to get any help or explanation from him. Taki, unfazed, lifted her eyes to meet mine, her face radiating irritation.

"Speak your peace and get the fuck out of my house," she spat, her tone drenched in venom, before closing her eyes as if relishing her power over the situation.

I let out a small breath, my frustration mounting, but I had come here with a purpose – not to allow her theatrics or twisted games to derail me. Clearing my throat, I anchored my focus on the task at hand. Taki needed to understand the gravity of the situation, whether or not she cared to listen.

"Taki," I started, my voice steady but firm, "your team is hotter than a goddamn inferno right now. We've lost too many workers, and now government officials are swarming Atlanta like fleas on a damn dog. Your name? It's all over the CIA's radar, hosting music on their radio waves. Hell, Rude Boy running wild on his rampage hasn't helped either. You can't tell me you don't see how this mess affects us both. If this chaos keeps spiraling, neither of us comes out alive in this game. The deal we made? It's going up in flames, and to top it off, I haven't received my money yet." I leaned forward slightly, my tone sharpened. "You need to rein in your people and figure out who the hell keeps leaking information, or this whole arrangement is going to crash and drag all of us straight down the drain."

For a moment, Taki ignored me completely, continuing her disturbing escapade like my words were no more than background noise. Then, without breaking stride, she slowly gazed up at me, her mouth slightly gapping as she grabbed hold of the man's head and grinded her pussy in his face, cumming hard. Her body racked and thighs trembled as her breathing became erratic, and she bit her bottom lip. I was annoyed but couldn't help the hard on I was getting in my pants from watching. Taki went limp, and her breathing was back to normal, as she slowly rubbed the guy's head. Whoever he was, I could tell he had did a good job of pleasing her. She seemed satisfied.

I cleared my throat. "Taki…"

Taki sat up with the quickness and locked eyes with me with an icy calm that sent chills up my spine. "You don't think I know who's talking on my side of the field?" she asked, her voice low and eerie, each word deliberate. "I've got every man in place for a reason, Mason."

As if to emphasize her control, she tightened her legs around the man's neck – the same guy who had been buried between her thighs minutes before. He struggled violently now, gasping for air, while two of her guards sprang forward, grabbing his hands and locking them in cuffs. Despite his frantic twisting and thrashing, the motion was immediately subdued as Taki's hold grew stronger.

The man screamed, desperate for breath, but Taki's legs squeezed tighter like a vice, cutting off his air circulation entirely. The room seemed to grow quieter, heavier, with each agonizing second of his struggle.

"See, Mr. Mason," Taki continued, her words cold and detached, "this man here actually got the chance to live his life before he died. Lucky for him, tasting me was one of his final pleasures. Not everyone gets to savor death like this. But betrayal?" Her gaze pierced mine as she spoke. "Even in the afterlife, he's not going to outrun what's coming for him."

The man writhed for a few more moments, his movements growing weaker, until his body finally went limp. My stomach knotted as I watched her hold him in place, even in death, as if to savor his lifeless form. A full minute passed before she relaxed her hold, letting his limp body flop to the floor like discarded trash.

Unbothered and unashamed, Taki stood up. Naked, bold, and utterly unapologetic, she didn't bother to cover herself – not with arms, not with clothes, not with shame. Instead, she strolled over to the coffee table where a rolled cigar sat, waiting. With an almost theatrical ease, she lit it, letting the embers glow brightly, then took a slow drag, blowing out a thick cloud of smoke that hung heavy in the air.

I looked at her, my mind racing between fear and disbelief. Taki's version of power wasn't just raw; it was ruthless, unfiltered, and terrifyingly calculated. There wasn't even the smallest flicker of remorse in her eyes.

This woman was chaos incarnate, and somehow, I had tied myself to her.

Taki exhaled another thick cloud of smoke, her posture relaxed despite the lifeless man now lying on the floor. She turned her sharp, unwavering gaze back to me, her tone now dripping with icy confidence.

"My rat is dead," she said coldly, gesturing casually to the body as if it were little more than a nuisance she'd dealt with. "I've been watching him for weeks before you even suspected anything, Mr. Mason. So spare me the lectures. I already knew his betrayal was brewing before you showed up here to tell me what you think you've figured out." She leaned forward slightly, her nakedness adding an unsettling edge to her words. "I'm not sure you fully understand what's happening. Rude Boy wants to see me fall – but let me make something very clear. I didn't claw my way to the top just to bend or break for him. Not for you. Not for the senator. Not for that fool CIA agent running around playing hero. None of them matter to me. Because in the end, Mason, everyone loses before I crumble."

The sharpness in her voice hit me like a slap. Her words weren't empty bravado; they were declarations of war spoken by a woman who'd burned bridges and built empires. For a moment, I studied her, trying to gauge just how far she'd take this and how long I could afford to risk staying in her orbit. But I couldn't let her insatiable drive to win destroy everything we'd built.

I steadied myself as I replied, keeping my composure intact. "I get that your feelings are on the table, Taki. You're being upfront, and I respect that. But let me remind you of one thing – we have a multi-million-dollar roundtable riding on the foundation we've built together. That table keeps all of us in positions of power, and if it collapses, everyone goes with it. You wouldn't even have a seat at the table if it weren't for me. I helped you secure your place. So, answer me this – where does that leave me?"

Taki's lips curled into a faint smirk, the kind that spoke of disdain and amusement all at once. She took another drag from the cigar and blew the smoke upward, as if discarding my words in the plumes.

"It leaves you exactly where you need to be, Mason," she said, her voice even but steely, laced with an unyielding resolve. "You talk about winning, but you're delusional if you think there's ever going to be a winner in all of this." She stood straighter now, looking me dead in the eyes, daring me to challenge her. "This war? It doesn't have an end. Rude Boy's fighting for something he'll never let go of, and I'm fighting for something I never had – something I should've gotten years ago. And I'll die before I stop fighting for it."

Her words hung in the air heavily, a mix of fury and determination. That was the problem with Taki. She wasn't just fighting battles; she was fighting purpose itself, fighting to mend whatever scars or voids had fueled her ambition to dominate. But the collateral damage piling up around her? That didn't mean a damn thing in her eyes. To her, it was just evidence of her determination. And that made her all the more dangerous to everyone involved – including me.

~

Rude Boy
District 17
The Black Cartel

The sun was dipping low, its golden hues fading as the first whispers of night began to spill across the sky. I was flying down the highway, doing the dash like I was racing against time. My outfit was sharp but lowkey. – Steve Madden button-down, Balenciaga jeans, and instead of my usual designer kicks, I was rocking a clean pair of cocaine white Air Force Ones. My destination was District 17, the kind of place where legends were made – or broken. I was on my way to meet with The Black Cartel, the undisputed kings of the south. They ran Georgia like a well-oiled machine, touching every drug deal, every high-end car sale, every designer outfit sold in the streets. Even the best clubs, restaurants, and nightlife hotspots carried their fingerprints. Everyone knew you didn't move weight or money in their territory without cutting them a piece of the action. They weren't just untouchable; they were the ones pulling strings nobody even knew existed.

Right now, I needed their power and influence more than ever. Our business wasn't just about transactions; it was about leverage and survival. Taki, one of my loose ends, was out here flipping the game on its head. She was holding a rock – not just any problem but the kind that could turn cordial deals into blood-stained chaos. Her slick moves were threatening to upend everything, making enemies out of allies and playing a dangerous game with my peoples' lives. I knew The Black Cartel was my ticket to shutting her down. Their reach was vast, their network unmatched. What I needed was an in – someone in their ranks who could be persuaded, someone who could move the chessboard in my favor.

This wasn't just business. This was survival, clean and simple. If I wanted to send Taki and her chaos to an early grave, I'd need the kind of power only The Black Cartel could offer. Tonight, deals would be cut, lines would be crossed, and the course of my future – and Taki's – would be decided.

I pulled into the driveway slowly, double-checking the GPS to confirm that I was at the right address. When dealing with these people, details mattered; they had a reputation for being particular about everything from appearances to timing to the smallest aspects of business. It was something I respected about them. This wasn't just any family; they were a family that carried their reputation with pride, the kind of Black excellence that set the bar for everyone looking on.

Stepping out of my car, I took a moment to straighten my blazer before making my way to the grand front door. The house itself was a masterpiece, sprawling and immaculate, radiating an air of old-money elegance and new-money shine. When I rang the doorbell, the response came swiftly.

The door swung open to reveal a white butler, dressed sharply in a black and white suit. He looked like he'd been plucked from the pages of a James Bond novel. "Mr. Bah, Mr. Bentley is waiting for you in the dining area," he announced smoothly, stepping aside to let me pass.

I nodded my thanks, stepping across the threshold into a home that exuded wealth and power. The interior was even more magnificent than I imagined with vaulted ceilings, gleaming marble floors, and artwork that looked like it belonged in a museum. If I accepted what Payne Bentley was about to propose, my life could change dramatically, but the weight of that decision wasn't lost on me, even surrounded by such opulence.

"Rude Boy, what a pleasure to have you here, my brother. It's been too long," Payne Bentley greeted me warmly as I entered the dining area. From his seat at the head of the long, polished mahogany table, he radiated charisma and authority. His smile was flawless, the kind that set people at ease – and put them on edge at the same time.

Payne wasn't just the patriarch of this household; he was a force to be reckoned with in Atlanta's power circles. A major entrepreneur with pockets deep enough to fund half the city, he had investments in everything from real estate to education and construction projects. His influence reached as far as the political sphere, ensuring that officials were eager to keep him happy. Sitting at his table were a handful of his family members, and standing at unobtrusive intervals around the room, three armed guards kept watch, their presence a quiet reminder of what it took to maintain this lifestyle.

"Take a seat, brother. We're about to eat," he said, gesturing to an empty chair near his side.

I walked over and sat down, the rich aroma of the food making my stomach turn traitor. Payne nodded toward a woman standing off to the side, dressed in a crisp uniform. "Sarah, fix him a plate," he said.

The waitress, Sarah, moved quickly to my side, her movements efficient yet polished. She poured me a glass of champagne with practiced precision, her dark eyes meeting mine for a brief moment that ended in a quick wink before she disappeared back to the kitchen.

The table was laden with dishes that looked like they belonged in a five-star restaurant – a decadent spread of fish, steak, bowls of creamy pasta, stuffed fried crab, and more. Platters of asparagus and perfectly arranged sushi kabobs took their place alongside fresh bread rolls and a vibrant salad. Everything was a visual feast, and it was clear no expense was spared in the preparation.

A moment later, Sarah returned with a light plate she'd prepared for me. I accepted it with a polite nod and picked up my fork. Taking a small bite of the fish, I was greeted with a flavor so rich and perfectly seasoned that it took me by surprise. Despite the critical thoughts lingering in the back of my mind about why I was really here, I let myself focus – for now – on the extraordinary meal in front of me. Something told me the conversations to follow would demand my full attention.

"This is very thoughtful of you," I started, eyeing the expensive meal laid out before him. "But, to be honest, I came here tonight because I need your help." There was no point in beating around the bush.

He paused mid-bite and flashed a faint, almost amused smile. "My help?" He chuckled lightly, leaning back in his chair. "Rude Boy, why would you need my help? Things are going great on my end. Meanwhile, your city... Well, it's chaos as usual." He returned to his meal with a slow precision, savoring each bite. "I hear the cops are even starting to poke their noses around again. Hopefully not anywhere near where my money's being made though."

I shook my head, my tone hard as steel. "I can assure you money is the least of your concerns if we can't reach an understanding tonight. Taki's gone rogue — wild even. She's broken the codes of our city, something I can't tolerate. I plan to get rid of her. She's been running your traffic for cocaine and ecstasy across all her districts, but it's time for that to change. I'm offering to take over her operations. My men will handle it from now on, and I'll personally make sure your profits keep coming in — on top of my payment to you for this round. My crew is just as strong, just as connected, as hers and more reliable."

Mr. Bentley set his fork down, dabbing at the corners of his mouth with a crisp, white napkin before leaning back in his chair. The subtle clink of his silverware against the plate echoed in the room. "That's quite an offer," he mused, looking at me with a mix of curiosity and skepticism. "A lot to spring on someone after we haven't seen each other in God knows how long. And while I'll admit Taki has been unraveling for a while now – something we both knew would happen eventually – it doesn't mean I care who's in charge of those districts." He gestured lazily, like his words were as casual as the conversation. "What matters to me is that the numbers keep adding up. I'm not here to play favorites. Don't forget, Rude Boy," his voice dropped slightly as he fixed me with a sharp look, "I don't care about you either. But considering you hold the future of my finances in your hands, why don't you lay it out properly before I make any assumptions?"

I leaned forward, locking eyes with him. "I'm talking about more than Taki. I want your help taking her down *and* the senator. This is bigger than the usual shit. You and your men would be instrumental in this."

Bentley's brow lifted, and for a moment, there was silence – just the sound of the silverware as he resumed eating. Finally, he set his fork down again, a deep chuckle rumbling from his chest. "You've completely lost your mind." His voice held admiration, despite the disbelief in his words. "And honestly, I like it. Taking down Taki? Fine. She's burned enough bridges to justify it, and I even have a few addresses you can visit to get the ball rolling. Just don't make a mess too close to my operation. I don't need heat." He paused for a moment, his eyes narrowing as he spoke again. "But as for the senator? That's a different beast entirely. I can't touch him. If I so much as breathe in his direction, I'll spend the rest of my life behind bars. That's your problem to handle. I'll lend you my men for Taki, but you're on your own for the senator. Keep it lowkey though. I know you're on a mission."

He picked up his fork again, the clink of metal hitting porcelain signaling the end of the discussion in his mind.

"That's much appreciated, bro," I said, standing up. "I gotta get my girl back, mon. This ain't just business. It's personal."

Bentley nodded, the weight of my words not fully registering on his face. "That's on you," he replied bluntly. "I don't know, nor do I care, what the situation is between you two. That's not my concern. I'll have everything you need by tomorrow."

He paused and held up his hand before I could leave. "One more thing, Rude Boy."

I stopped and turned. "Yeah?"

"If this senator business becomes my problem…" He leaned back in his chair, his voice calm but laced with quiet menace, "that's gonna be a major issue for you."

I met his gaze, keeping my face neutral. The warning hung in the air like a weight, but I didn't flinch. I understood the stakes. I didn't take the threat lightly, but I didn't let it shake me either. There was too much on the line. I had a mission to accomplish, one that couldn't afford distractions or hesitation. I was determined to connect every piece, and when the time came, this city would burn, along with everyone who stood in the way.

"Understood," I replied, my voice steady.

With that, I turned and walked out of the kitchen. The house was as silent as when I'd first entered, only the soft sound of my footsteps filling the space. Stepping out into the night air, I felt a strange sense of relief sweep over me. The cool breeze brushed against my face as I made my way down the driveway, a reminder that one chess piece had finally fallen into place. But the game wasn't over – not by a long shot.

Reaching into my jacket, I pulled out my phone and dialed Ghost's number. I leaned against my car as the ringtone buzzed in my ear. He didn't make me wait long.

"Let me guess," he answered without a "hello." His tone was sharp, impatient. "I don't need to come around the corner, huh?"

"Nah," I said, smirking at his bluntness. "He's actually helping us willingly. Turns out nobody likes that bitch. We just need to lay low, keep things quiet, and wait for the right moment to take her out."

"Waiting?" Ghost cut in, his frustration bleeding through the receiver. "Waiting has gotten us exactly nowhere, Rude Boy. Nowhere."

Before I could get in a word of reassurance, he hung up on me. Classic Ghost – always aiming to hit fast and hard and rarely interested in nuance.

I let out a sigh, slipping the phone back into my pocket. As much as I didn't want to admit it, he wasn't wrong. Time wasn't on our side, and we couldn't afford to drag this out longer than necessary. This needed to be executed flawlessly, but there was no room for delays – not anymore.

Sliding into the driver's seat, I gripped the wheel, my mind racing as I stared out at the road ahead. The district wasn't far, but the gap between the present moment and the endgame felt like a lifetime. As I pulled out of the driveway, I could feel the tension growing, the weight of the mission pressing down on me. I began mentally shortening the timeframe, already strategizing my next move, knowing that hesitation would only get me killed.

It was time to get everything in order. And when the time came, Taki – and anyone protecting her – would fall.

AGENT JAMIYAH PORTER

ude Boy was focused on going head-to-head with this bitch, Taki. I didn't know as much as he did, but I knew we didn't need to give her any time to think or any time to form another deadly plan because we might not get so lucky with walking away the next time.

We were being followed by a crew from the state of New York, and it was not clear exactly what objectives they had in mind. I couldn't say how it would end, going into this district to approach Mendez's territory for any reason at all. The most blood had been shed between Districts 5 and 7. We needed help, and if these people decided to step any differently, this would more than likely end up being a shootout.

Making our way down to the end of District 7, we could see District 5 mounted up at the edge of their territory. I hated to see face-offs like this because there was never any guarantee on how things would turn out. We needed to break this city apart from Taki, and that was the only sure leverage we had in getting his family back in one piece.

"We aren't debating with these motherfuckers. Either they are helping or just sitting to the side, awaiting their funeral. No tolerance from this day forward," Rude Boy announced before stepping out of the truck.

Zeus and his crew were nearly out of the car before us, and I didn't need him crushing out the chances of District 5 joining sides with us to take this bitch down. I quickly motioned for JoJo to stay close to me and Rude Boy as we met up at the borderline with this crazy ass Mexican.

"Well, if it isn't the weasel that killed my fucking cousin. Surprised you had the nuts to come out here, man!" The head honcho spoke, holding his gun in his hand.

He was backed by at least an army of twenty men, but you could see that not everybody was happy to be there at the moment. Zeus and his crew stood by silently as Rude Boy cleared his throat to speak.

"Listen, loco ass nigga. I spoke with your people on the phone, and I'll say this shit again. I'm not responsible for Mendez dying. District 7 did more than business on cocaine when it came down to him, so I believe I lost more than just money on that end. I'm not the problem, but if you would like to join us in burying all of them, we wouldn't have to debate about who killed who," he tried to reason with him.

"Join you for what? We can barely even trust our own to remain loyal to the district. It's a rude awakening coming to you soon because we aren't the only ones invested in this bloodshed. You are behind so many people losing their lives that the Reaper himself is looking for you. Tizo's father needs answers as well about his son being murdered in a cell that your associate has ties with. It's only a matter of time before she tries to come take what's left of us, and then we lose all around the board."

"Fuck this!" Zeus spat before raising his gun, killing the Mexican who stood the closest to him.

Poc!

I watched his head splatter, and within seconds, all guns were drawn, and the Hispanics were in a panic.

"Let's get something fucking straight. Lower the guns or we will all die. We didn't come here this morning to be taunted and disrespected. Your help was asked for because we wish to get to the bottom of this. Just as you have lost people on your side, we have suffered casualties as well. If you wish for there to be no more killing, I suggest you figure out every way to possibly help us get this bitch's head in our hands, so we all can rest easy," Zeus spoke calmly.

The Mexicans stood quietly, staring back and forth between one another, and you could see the fear written on their faces. Atlanta was a dog nation, and if you weren't prepared to die in the fight, you were done before the battle even began.

"You make quite a fucking impression for us to be standing at the same position with this bitch. District 5 helping you does what? She's killed nearly half of the town. What makes you feel that you can do anything different from us?" he asked, looking back and forth between Rude Boy and Zeus.

"Because we have no other option, and I'm sure that we can do many things on our own that you aren't capable of. This isn't the time to worry about who is better and worse at what we're dealing with. I just need the extra force you have to back us with, cutting this problem loose. Either we stand together or we can go ahead and just end this misunderstanding right here and now," Rude offered in a moderate tone.

He scurried over his thoughts, and I could tell that he didn't have too many options on his hands to decide from. We all needed room to protect our own, but he stood exactly beside us when it came down to deleting Taki from existence.

"So, what's next then, since all this shit seems to be so figured out?"

"Easy," Rude Boy replied. "We knock down these crooked cops, and we murder every soul that decides to stand next to this bitch. I look at it like this. We have forty-eight hours to handle our affairs before we all-out purge this soil. Let's make the best out of this shit because if I don't get my family back, I'll be fixing my dirt bed right here. The next stop is District 9 with the Rastafari. They work hand in hand with her, and if we can get them to respect what we are standing on, we can move with strength instead of stupidity. So, I'll make this clear. Allow District 5 to stay open for our use, and we will walk away from this dictatorship together. Does that sound like a deal?"

The head Mexican stared into Rude Boy's eyes. I didn't know if he wanted to refuse or not, but the opportunity that was just laid out surely wasn't going to be around for long. It was time to take advantage while we had it.

"We're in, but don't say that I didn't warn you that this shit would get everybody killed," he agreed before allowing us to cross over the border into District 5.

FBI CHIEF MASON

It was around the afternoon when I found myself driving down the expressway along the outskirts of Atlanta. The inside of the Fulton County walls and counties were a dead zone compared to the outside sources that had more power and connections than just the inside of the warzone. The city structure was defined by the elite people who could find whatever they wanted to see happen. Those people were the ones behind the scenes, the ones who made it possible for government officials like me to move around these cold-blooded killers and not have a hair on my head touched.

Turning into District 11, I crossed the line into DeKalb County and was sure to straighten out my rearview. You had to be aware in this territory with hoodlums and even the civilians because this was the district that could easily trick you if you weren't aware of your surroundings. District 11 was built on prostitution, distribution of cocaine, and some of the best entertainment services that a person could find – rappers, pornography, restaurants, and much more that could bring in an easy dollar. Of course, it was mainly populated by the Caucasian people, and the niggas were a small minority made to live in the slum sides of DeKalb, sectioned away from the royalty if you may call it.

Pulling up to the large steel gate, I stopped at the camera monitor and pushed the voice button on the box. It didn't take long for a man's tone to come through the speaker.

"The Pomellos' residence. State your identity please."

"Hey, good morning, uh, whoever I'm speaking with. My name is Chief Mason from the Federal Bureau of Investigation. I'm here to see if I could speak with Mr. Pomello if he's in by chance."

The monitor went silent, and after about three minutes of waiting for an answer, I was prepared to push the monitor again and make my position known. Never in a day would a criminal undermine me in my city, especially when I came in peace. I was willing to go the extra mile to keep my bank account and my authority safe because the CIA was sure to bring everyone down who placed a finger into a decision inside of Atlanta.

Before I could make my move, the sound of the gates began to open, allowing me to pull my car inside of the home's parking lot. I had to admit that you didn't see too many people who could afford a true palace like the one I was sitting in, but it wasn't special when you had a multi-million-dollar family that pushed their weight around as much as possible. When the Pomellos had a problem, people died. No one would see how or when, but their dirty work would always be handled.

I went to turn off my engine and step out of my car. Before I could even place my two feet on the ground, there was a bundle of armed men beaming down around my doors – six of them with assault rifles. None of them seemed to be violent. None of them spoke. I received a nod from one of the men who looked to be in charge, and since I hadn't been seen yet, this was my invitation to come inside and see what I could figure out.

I didn't want to walk into a nasty situation, but this was the only way I would find out exactly what was next to happen. I was led through the front door of the property and escorted straight to a back-yard deck that was surrounded by at least two acres of land and a variety of vehicles that were parked off to the side on a lengthy drive-way. The first car I noticed was a grey 2024 Rolls Royce Spectre. Sitting directly beside it was my dream car, a royal indigo 2024 Aston Martin DBX 707. Just two of this motherfucker's cars were worth

$750,000, not including the toys and collectibles that weren't in eye's view.

Stepping up to the porch, I spotted Mr. Pomello and his wife sitting by the pool as if it were a day of relaxation and comfort. I wasn't used to making this type of approach with underworld criminals, but it was more than necessary to get to an understanding.

"Good evening, Mr. Pomello. Agent Mason."

He removed his shades before staring down at his gold Rolex Submariner watch.

"Indeed, I've never had a federal agent get the guts to step foot on my property unless they were trying to accuse me of something. I mean, of course, nothing could ever touch a family like this – not the government, not the bottom feeding thugs around this minefield. What the fuck possessed you to step foot on my property without alerting me beforehand? And what makes you feel that you will walk out the same way you came?" he asked me before sipping from the small shot glass in his hand.

I had to catch myself before replying and making a move that I could regret. I was standing on the land of one of the most ruthless families in the state of Georgia.

"I can assure you that I will leave the same way I came, or my people will ensure that you end up the way I leave. I'm not here to make enemies with you, nor bring disrespect to your doorsteps, but the major problems that we have on our hands right now is causing grief and pain in this town, and you may be my only help in putting this to an end. Your uncle is on a rampage, and he's not caring who's affected by his irrational behavior while using his power. He's the fucking senator of the state, and he moves like El Chapo."

"I have nothing to do with anything that my uncle does anymore. I told you that I'm not a part of that life. I'm a legit businessman, and quite frankly, I don't even like being approached about this. You telling me you can't handle an old man like my uncle?"

"No, I can handle anything that comes my way, but I don't think this situation will be normal. We have a war on our hands, and I don't think we're ready to lose any more blood on these streets because it may be bad for us all. The streets and the law."

"And why should I care about any of that? Me and my wife have our own family objectives to attend to. I just told you that I have nothing to do with him. So, what are you talking about?"

"I'm speaking on him inquiring about this kid. Who the fuck is he?"

I could see the switch in his energy when I mentioned the boy. He sat up straight, removing the shades from his face.

"What boy?"

"That's what I'm asking you. This war has spiraled downhill for a lot of us, and we don't need the heat that's about to fall upon this entire operation. This kid is the source of the problem from what I'm piecing together. This is the reason I'm standing in your home this morning. Maybe you can tell me better than what I'm understanding."

Mr. Pomello stood up and closed the distance in between us.

"That kid that you speak of has been missing for over five years, and he happens to be my cousin. Now, before we get on a delicate subject, I would warn you not to speak on anything that you don't know to be true. Yes, this world between me and my uncle is closed, but if you're speaking on my cousin being alive after all this time, we might actually have something to talk about." He looked me square in the eyes.

"I'll tell you this, Mr. Pomello. He's very much alive, but the catastrophic shit that your uncle has raining down on Atlanta, he may not be able to make it back to you guys safely."

"You need to tell me exactly what you know and need, and if this is true, what you say about my cousin being alive, I'll give you all the assistance needed." He held out his hand to seal the deal.

"Is there anywhere private where we can talk?"

"Come inside," he offered before walking me into the home.

∽

Agent Wilburn
District 7

It was getting to the middle of the day, and my mind was set on finding everyone I could at the top of my list. It was said that this city was unbreakable. I had a down pat game on how I approached the streets when I needed to know something. I always got what I wanted in the end. I rode through the streets, witnessing the heathens that walked about and posted in front of establishments. The thugs had literally taken over the entire city, and they were not beyond applying oppression on the neighborhoods.

I made a few calls to some colleagues that were good at going against anyone. We were bred to track down stupid idiots and put them under. It was the reason I'd risen in the ranks of the CIA. I would stop at nothing.

Pulling into the old Club Lucky parking lot, I parked my car in the back and stepped out. The air smelled like piss, and I knew for a fact that the Wolf Gang had to be near from the graffiti that was on the concrete and trash cans. I was set to meet up with an informant that was giving us intel on the Wolf Gang but mainly their leader, some guy named Rude Boy. He boiled my blood to the core. I'd dealt with plenty of men like him in my days, and I always happened to come out on top.

Stepping up to the door, I hit the buzzer and knocked on the burglar bar door. I turned my head back-and-forth to watch my surroundings. I could never be too careful. After two minutes of lingering around, the locks shifted, and he stuck his head out. Keenan used to make runs for one of Rude Boy's trap spots. One of the main supporters of his organization, he was known in all the lower districts for his supply and demand. No one could out race him when it came to the distribution game. He was never off beat. He was also the name that came up on my list to find if I needed to know anything. According to the streets, Keenan owed Rude Boy a good amount of money that was never reimbursed. It clearly looked as if he had to hide out at certain times of the day because I'd never seen a pure hustler in this city have to do their dealings in private.

"You must be Agent Wilburn?"

"Clearly."

I looked around the empty parking lot as if we weren't the only two standing around. Even though I could sense nervousness all over him, he allowed me to enter the shop, closing the burglar bar door behind me. The inside of the club was still clean and in great condition, but you could tell that it hadn't been in business for a while with actual guests.

Keenan moved across the floor, back over to the bar, where he was before letting me in. There were over six empty liquor bottles lying around, and clearly, the open drug packaging alerted me that he had been obviously sitting around, getting loaded, as he waited for his death to appear.

"So, what all do I owe you, and I'm not willing to talk all goddamn day. I only agreed to this because your agents promised they could get me out of this city with no problems on the backend. Now, if we can't make that shit right there come back like crack, I don't think we need to be talking about smack." He threw back a shot glass of tequila before looking at me.

I pulled a chair out from the bar and sat down next to him. I knew how a vulnerable person felt when they had no way out. It was terrifying, and that was my reason for comforting him to find out exactly what I needed to know.

"Keenan, you don't owe me a damn thing. I'm here simply because I have a job to do. If you owe anybody anything, you owe it to yourself. We both know that the gangs here in this city has overthrown people that shouldn't have been overstepped. I'm here because I need names, and I need this shit to end with this government and citizens. Atlanta wasn't built for the residents in the area to war with the people. These idiots that you've came out here and slaved over have placed a chokehold on the same neighborhoods that raised them up. Rude Boy was close to you from what I hear. Not too sure about Taki, but I'm sure there may be something that I can catch from you unless you want to catch the back of a cell or the bottom of a ditch."

I knew that my statement had gotten him right because he was starting to fidget around nervously.

"Listen, Rude Boy has always been the same. Yeah, he runs part of Atlanta and has always held a position, but times are getting different down here now. Taki isn't shit to play with. Her reputation for getting a person hurt is the key to keeping the press on all her associates. She forces you to do business with her districts, and after she feels like you aren't holding your end of the bargain good enough, she replaces you with another sitting duck. If that bitch ain't stopped soon, I'm not sure what will be the fate of this city," Keenan stressed, downing another shot.

"I'm confused here. I'm hearing in the streets that all these people were once on the same team. You telling me friends and loved ones out here killing each other for power and money?"

He looked at me and smirked.

"No. For love."

"What?"

"Exactly what I said. People are dying, and business is going downhill because motherfuckers are fueling of one another. I quit working for Rude after he pistol whipped me about forty thousand dollars getting stolen. He did that shit in front of a room full of bitches. He made sure he always put on for a bitch and Shanti. Now, this same shit you love so much got everybody falling to hell. The best thing for you to do is leave these people alone because they're gonna crash themselves out. I don't associate with anybody anymore. That's why I'm secluded out here." He grabbed the bottle for a third time, and I was slightly getting my cue to leave.

"Taki is the leader of district 13 and 1. The Wolf crew holds territory in 12 and 7, correct?"

He nodded.

"Taki owns a lot of territory now. You wanna find her head, just go through the toughest projects."

I took that bit of information and headed for the back door. Letting myself out, I pondered on what Keenan had just told me. My eyes were so good that I caught the sight of someone standing not too far in front of me, and I quickly lifted my head. The young, white kid held a black semi-automatic AR-15 in his palm. A hoodie was tied tightly over his head, and before I could think about reaching for my gun, he was squeezing his trigger.

Ploc! Ploc! Ploc! Ploc! Ploc! Ploc!

I ran for my life and slid right across the concrete behind my car.

Snatching my gun from my hip, I aimed over the hood of my car and released fire back.

Boc! Boc! Boc! Boc!

The sound of a rampage of bullets smacked the side of my car, forcing me to duck again. I could feel the glass from my shattered windows falling over my head before the fire came to a cease.

I took a deep breath, slowing down my thoughts. Backup was out of the question, and I refused to allow these idiots to trap me before I could arrest their entire neighborhood.

I jumped to my feet with my gun aimed, and he was nowhere in sight. I moved slowly around my car and couldn't help but message my crew to meet at the headquarters. Looking at my bullet riddled car, I was still able to climb in and pull away from my current origin. I needed to make it back to my perimeter, and the hunt could surely begin. In all my days in law enforcement, I had never been run away by a killer, because I was one myself for sure, and I had a team of men that were exactly the same.

~

District 13
College Park
Seven Hours Later

After I gathered my team of men, we geared up and headed over for clearance by the judge. The first territory that was being taken by the government was District 13 by choice or force. We didn't come to speak, neither did we accept thugs shooting at cops. My crew consisted of my retired military brothers. There was Olson, the technician, Randy was an expert mercenary and Navy seal, and Lott was an ex-cop, marital arts trained with time secured in the military. I trusted these men with my life, and I knew if I had to risk going in for the sake of the people, I could count on them.

We were two vehicles strong with a small backup crew right around the corner in case. The home was a local drug spot for the Kiss Squad members. It was heard that Taki made her runs through the loca-

69

tion throughout the week, and if it was a place of income and suspects, we were coming in.

After loading our guns and securing the perimeter, I counted the men out front and noticed a few more lingering further down the street.

"Guys, we going in and arresting everything moving. If they get violent, kill them, no hesitation. We are the law, and in order to end this bullshit, we have to be fast and efficient. On three. Three!" I shouted before we jumped out the truck in unison.

My rifle was aimed in front of me, and my boys were directly behind me. By the time we crossed the street, we were spotted, and I heard the stress call yelled.

"Cops! Police! Police!"

Men started to scatter, and we immediately saw the wrong thing when a guy raised a gun. I immediately took him down with two shots to the chest.

Boom! Boom!

He dropped, and the fire started to erupt. A few of them tried to get off a shot, but my guys were fast, taking another two out of their misery before we barged through the front gate, heading for the door. One hard kick and it was lying against the wall inside the home.

"Let's go! Get on the fucking ground or you die!" I yelled, rushing into the living room area where three people were standing.

My team split up, and I forced the group to the ground by cuffing each one. My eyes were on every part of this death hole because shit could go wrong at any moment.

After ten minutes, my team was walking back up front. A total of seven people were arrested, and it was probably one of the biggest drug and cash busts that the government had ever seen. It was too bad they would never find out about it. With dedication came hard work.

I walked around, looking at the people we arrested, and all of them seemed like regular citizens from the neighborhood – normal men and women who looked as if they were truly struggling.

"One of you are going to have to give me some information, or all of you are going down forever." I rotated my eyes between them.

They all sat quietly for a second, and a young female came forward.

"You can't stop her. She has killed everyone in the neighborhood. The police are scared of her. You can't protect us either." She folded her arms as if all hope for humanity was over.

I shook my head and called in a squad of backup to come seal off the place and get the people who needed it to safety, being sure that the authorities placed surveillance on this spot. We would ensure that no more Kiss Squad members stepped in this area.

TAKI

I spread my legs, feeling Vince slide inside me, but each thrust did little to satisfy me. Sweat dripped down my back, and frustration built with every second. If I didn't catch a nut soon, I was going to lose it; maybe even snap on him.

"Damn, Vince, you feel like you're just here to generate heat, not pleasure," I muttered, exasperated.

He tried to step up, switching up his rhythm, but the more he tried, the more annoyed I got. No matter how many positions we flipped through, none of them brought any relief. Finally, I pushed him off, letting out a heavy sigh.

"I'm done. You're decent, but not good enough to make me feel like the sun is laid out on my chest."

Vince rolled to the side, catching his breath, and looked at me with wounded pride. "Damn, Taki, you ain't got to play me like that. I didn't think I was that bad."

Ignoring him, I climbed out of bed and walked straight to the mini bar. I poured myself a shot of Hennessy, tossed it back, and started weighing my options. Vince followed, hovering near, and that's when a thought clicked in my mind.

"It's funny how close you've gotten to me, so quickly," I said, turning to face him. "You put in work for this crew, but shit is getting deeper now. So I gotta ask—how far are you willing to go for Kiss Squad?"

Vince's face turned serious. "As far as I have to, Taki. I know those other dudes have disappointed you, but I'm not like them. Just tell me what needs to be done."

"The senator has to go," Taki said, voice low but edged with menace. Around us, the dull hum of the club carried the secrets of Atlanta's underbelly—money exchanging hands, deals sealed over cocktails and cutthroat ambition. "Ever since he started poking his nose in our business, the flow from the cocaine and prostitution tables has flipped. I swear, numbers are down, and it's all because he wants what he wants and thinks he can force my hand. We run Atlanta. The minute he's out of the picture, I control these ports—the rest falls in line. Rude Boy won't have a choice but to come crawling, begging for mercy, for his family's safety." He let the threat linger, savoring it.

He had just declared war, but his energy faded when I raised the real question.

"You want me to kill the senator?" I asked, meeting his gaze.

He scowled, jaw clenched. "Did I fucking stutter?"

I held back a laugh, poured myself another shot, and swallowed it fast—liquid courage burning down my throat. "Taki, that's next level. Don't get it twisted, I'm not scared to handle business—but let's not pretend this is some random punk you can touch whenever. Senators roll with security, they got eyes everywhere. Hitting one isn't simple."

For a moment, silence hung thick in the air. He drummed his fingers on the table, impatient. "I don't care about his power or status. Anybody can be reached if you're smart about it. This is Kiss Squad, remember? Murder's our bread and butter. We send a message to anyone out in the outer districts—comply with our rules or face the consequences. If things get messy, the old man will make his move, but that's when you finish the job. No second chances."

"I got you," I said, nodding. The answer satisfied him, but I could tell he wanted more fire from me—more hunger for the kill. Commitment, not just compliance.

Still, my mind was already moving past the senator. Locking down Atlanta meant crushing every competitor, and I was done playing games with small-timers. Entertainment was for fools; I was here for dominance.

Rude Boy had drawn too much attention, stirred up chaos that spilled into my empire. Soon, he'd realize mercy would be a blessing —I could end him quick, or leave him trapped with me, powerless for eternity. That sick love he had for Shanti disgusted me, fueling my resolve. If I couldn't have him, no one could. Death was a mercy compared to what I had planned, and I was perfectly content with that thought.

~

JoJo
Westside District

I sat on the back porch of Abdullah's property in deep thought. Too much had occurred behind my insidious brother and his irrational behavior for the sake of power. It was a trait that he'd carried since I was a child coming up under him – a trait that my father encouraged instead of stopping. Now that he was dancing with the devil, the problem was now flushing from my dad's corner, and I was lost on what move to make. I couldn't allow Rude Boy and Shanti to fall because of my past.

The deep thought that I was going through at the moment was paused when Rude Boy stepped out of the patio door and gave me a curious look.

"How ya feel, mon? You know you're my little brother, and I can see when some shit is eating at you. I know you don't like outsiders around so much, but if this shit can be over within the next few days, we can leave and start over somewhere different. I just don't wanna take no chances with leaving this bitch alive. We'll never live in peace."

I looked into his eyes because, truthfully, I considered him a role model and true family, something that I begged to have when I was living under the roof of my father's home. The fast life and criminal world he lived in was what pushed me to drugs and to venture off on

74

my own inside the streets of Atlanta. My survival only stood firmly because of one reason – Rude Boy – giving me a chance.

"I feel like all of this is my fault, Rude. Shanti and her family wouldn't be going through this if I would have just listened and went back. I don't feel like that's my life anymore. When you picked me up at fifteen, I knew that I had somebody in my corner that actually wanted to be there. Me murdering everything in this world wouldn't change the fact that you are taking losses. I feel like if I go back, I might not have a chance to come out."

"JoJo, you're like a little brother to me, ya hear me? Nobody controls the shit that happens in this world. We can only take accountability for things in our control. Losing friends and family rips me down to pieces but having the few solid ones still standing beside me is even more of a better feeling. I know that I'm not alone. We about to end this once and for all, even if I have to stop everything in my corner to see it cease. It's gone too far. Still in all, don't take the blame for nothing. We'll figure this shit out together. Ya understand me?" He nudged my shoulder, trying to lighten my spirit.

"How do you suppose we do this?"

"That's exactly why I came to talk to you. I know you have the best eyes in our crew, and I gotta game plan that may help us out. I need everybody to be on one accord. Regardless of what happens or what takes place, promise me if anything happens to me, you'll make sure these girls are okay."

"What do you mean if anything happens to you, Rude Boy? We're together."

"JoJo, just promise me."

I looked at him, trying to find out what the reason for his statement was, but it was always a different spirit within Rude that others didn't understand. It was his heart that made him as solid as stone. I was willing to stand just as firm until the smokescreen cleared.

"I promise."

"Good, let me run it down to you how we coming then," he mentioned as we walked inside Abdullah's safe house.

VINCE

District 13

It was around 12:30 at night when I made my way out to District 13 for this group meet up. I loved being in charge of a crew like the Kiss Squad, but I hated having to slow down and coach niggas on how to be the best thugs they could be. I was making more money than I could count, and my name was stretched across Atlanta for handling the business when it came down to Taki's word. This was the shit I lived for, and now that we had a new agenda, I was going to ignite the city up with fuckery until all our problems fell. I linked ties with the Black Cartel. A few Cuban sources eventually came to abide after numerous men died from them denying our opportunity for business.

Once I arrived at my destination, I stepped out of my Cyber truck. Movement looked normal, and a few guests pushed through the parking lot, preparing for a good night out. I had called my young street runner earlier, alerting him about the meeting I was holding at our new property we owned, Club Foreign. It was only for reserved guests, and of course every leader that needed to make amends with Taki always had the avenue to do so.

Once I spotted this white boy, Kev, pulling up beside me, I waited until he exited his car to approach him. He sported a Ulysse Nardin watch. I knew the McLaren 650s he drove was the only one to touch Atlanta, and if you wanted more resources and open doors, Kev was the man to talk to. He wasn't the average white dude, but I wasn't the regular street killer. It was either our way or none. Taki wasn't accepting anything different. So, I was here today to force a choice out of this motherfucker. I just prayed he didn't take my approach as a choice because I was surely gonna make the final decision.

"Vince, good to see ya. How bout we get inside and grab a few drinks? Always good to have drinks during business." He flashed a fake smile that I wasn't buying.

Six of my Kiss Squad members were spread around the lot to keep a permanent eye out for anything that wasn't ordinary. I didn't need to slip or move around sloppy when I had this entire plan mapped out.

"I don't see why not. We already here," I replied, following behind him.

I always made sure we had extra security around the establishment on nights that were busy, but Club Foreign was one of the best invest-ments I could say I had ties with. Profits were more than large. We had a safe meet and greet for every big supplier in Georgia, not to mention the boss lady had a nasty press on anything that decided to step in her area. Kiss Squad was about to officially run the entire Atlanta.

After making our way inside, I nodded to the music as we moved through the building, straight for the back where the reserved area rested. Leather couches, bottles of champagne, and ice buckets were already in place, but this wasn't that type of greeting. It didn't take long for us to take a seat.

"So, wassup, Vince? I'm only in town for forty-eight hours, so I hope this can fit in between that schedule," he said before reaching into his pocket and pulling out an ounce of marijuana.

The audacity this little bitch had was crazy. He obviously didn't know we were on a dirt nap venture, and anybody could make the list, even a rapper's son like Kev.

I looked at my boys, giving them the signal that we were definitely gonna go with plan B and continued to address this dork ass muthafucka.

"Look, Kev, we're not gonna sit here and act like we haven't done similar business in the past. We just became friends over time, and that's always a possibility when it comes to money. Taki wants you to join teams. I mean, what harm can it do, you rockin' out with the baddest fuckin' crew in Atlanta?" I asked, not trying to be disrespectful.

He twisted his joint and sparked it before acknowledging my statement.

"Yes, we have done some business back in the day under some crazy conditions, but I would have to say that this isn't back in the day, Vince. I don't rock with the Kiss Squad because my district makes enough from pills and boosting. My car shops alone brings in more revenue than what Kiss Squad can offer me. Your people kill, okay. Mines do as well. If you don't have a business deal where I can profit a major capital off of, we really don't have shit to talk about. I can just enjoy my little vacay in the A and peel when I'm done."

"I just pulled out a red carpet and major respect, and you disrespect me as if I'm not talking about nothing. I wonder how Taki would feel about your response. You know the city is being raided by fucking cops. Standing alone wouldn't be a wise decision." I prepared myself for what I saw was about to happen.

He blew out a cloud of smoke and gave me an expression that said he didn't give a flying shit about what I was saying. From that point, I knew we were wasting our time. I needed the senator dead, and once he was gone, rules for us were nonexistent.

"Fuck Taki!" he spat with a nonchalant attitude.

"That's right." I smiled evilly.

Pulling out my Ruger 9x, I shot his first security in between the eyes, watching the soul leave his body before he touched the ground.

Boom!

Kev immediately choked on the small amount of smoke in his lungs as I aimed my gun at his second guard, pulling the trigger twice.

Boom! Boom!

The rest of my squad immediately started to handle everything around us and ignited the club to hit the exit. We weren't going anywhere. I didn't give a fuck who knew this piece of shit.

"I told you to take the deal."

I looked at him squirming on the floor, waiting for a response.

"You not taking nothing from me, Vince. You think everybody won't be out for your head."

Boom! Boom! Boom!

I shot his ass three times in the chest and quickly got the fuck up out of that bitch. Animosity wasn't the word on what was coming behind all the bloodshed. But it came with the territory and respect. The senator's ass was next on my list. I needed this move, and it needed to be done today.

ZEUS

After spending a week in the city, it started to feel like everything my family, my team, and I stood for was being disrespected – like our legacy, our bloodline, didn't carry the weight it deserved. Every encounter I'd had since setting foot in this place ended in violence. Not one person had the decency to give me clarity on what happened to my cousin, Yazi, but once my father made it my priority, there was no going back. His word was law. Handling it became my responsibility.

I wasn't exactly in a position to dive headfirst into chaos, but to get answers in a place like this, you had to be willing to make some noise. A quiet approach wasn't an option. I had requested – no, demanded – to be taken down to her district personally, wanting to handle it on my own terms. Whether she knew we were there or not wasn't the point. It was about catching her where she felt safe and unbothered. No one willingly allowed a group of killers into their territory to investigate problems – not without good reason. But I wasn't coming to ask politely. I wanted a face-to-face meeting, the kind that ended with her brains splattered against the wall. It was the only way I could get the satisfaction I needed.

The problem, though, was that this wasn't my domain. I was navigating unfamiliar terrain, and that left me at a disadvantage. Still, there was no turning back now.

"We're here," Rude Boy said as he killed the lights. His voice cut through the tense silence in the car like a blade.

I glanced out the window and assessed the situation. In front of the residence, a handful of workers were posted up. Some were armed, but most seemed oblivious to the world around them. They laughed, smoked, and moved with an air of confidence that bordered on recklessness. The Kiss Squad, the crew that ran this area, was too comfortable with their throne. They wore their power like a shield, leaving themselves exposed. That air of invincibility was their mistake. and it would become our opportunity. All we needed to do now was capitalize on it – by any means necessary.

"So, let me get this straight," I said, glancing at Rude Boy. "A woman has all this power over these men, right? Which means there's no point wasting time trying to talk to them. Might as well kill every last one of these clowns and force her to crawl out of hiding."

Rude Boy gave me a nod, his usual smirk spreading across his face. "Yeah, I'll keep that strategy in mind. But first, we gotta clear out all these liabilities around us. You know, make the space a little quieter." He leaned toward me slightly, nodding toward the nearby parking lot plaza. "I'll let you do the honors."

I shot him an unimpressed glance. "What's this supposed to be?"

He exhaled through his nose like he was explaining something obvious. "This here? It's the shopping plaza Taki raided about a year ago. Real low-life operation. She runs her girls out of the joint now — sells pussy like it's Black Friday."

My lip curled in disgust as I shook my head. "Wow. So, what? You need to stop in there for something? Better not be dragging me into some side errand."

"Nah, nothing like that." His tone dropped as he nodded toward a car parked in front of the plaza. "That Corvette over there, the old-school one? That's where it is. Three dudes posted inside. They're the guards for the girls inside. Basically, the eyes and the muscle. The driver's strapped. The front passenger – his name's Stiff. Second-in-command in her crew.

Oh, and just a little something for you: he's the one who helped Taki kill your cousin, Yazi. The dude in the backseat? He's unarmed. This is your moment – kill two birds with one stone while we got the chance."

He sat back in his seat, lit a joint, and took a long drag, like this was just another casual day for him.

Ghost stared at me from the passenger seat, probably expecting me to tell Rude Boy to step on it and drive off. But that kind of move wasn't in me anymore—not now.

Without a word, I popped my gun out of its holster, checked the magazine, and slipped it back into place. The air in the car was heavy. Too heavy. I stepped out, more focused than I'd been in days, and walked to the trunk. Using the foot sensor, I triggered it open. A small gas canister sat in the corner of the otherwise empty space. As I grabbed it, the trunk lowered, and I took a steadying breath. My energy shifted – relaxed, balanced. This would need precision — no rookie mistakes.

I moved across the street with deliberate calm. The late-night crowd barely noticed me. Just a few bystanders, probably watchers for Taki's crew, glanced my way but didn't intervene. They seemed to think I was just another passerby – just how I wanted it.

The Corvette was right where Rude Boy said it would be, its black exterior gleaming under the glow of the plaza lights. The windows were slightly tinted, but I could make out three figures inside, two in the front and one in the back. I knocked three times on the driver's window, bold and unapologetic.

The men inside were in the middle of a conversation, their hands moving animatedly as they spoke, but my knock yanked their attention. The driver turned his head, his brows furrowed in confusion, as he rolled the window down, annoyed but unprepared.

"Aye, you good, bro? What kinda idiot knocks on a window like this? Beat it, goofy," he said, waving me off like I was a pest.

I kept my tone calm, almost humble. "Sorry, man. I'm not trying to start anything. I'm just here about my cousin."

The driver's face twisted in a mix of irritation and confusion. "Your cousin? Who the fuck is your cousin?"

My hand found the pistol at my back. "Yazi."

The split second after his face shifted in recognition, I pulled the gun out and fired.

Boom!

The sound of the shot sliced through the night like thunder. The driver's head snapped to the side as the bullet connected with his skull. Blood sprayed like a violent wave inside the car. His limp body slumped against the wheel.

The crimson smear on the dashboard told the story before his body slumped against the steering wheel, lifeless. His brains painted a gruesome warning to the other two men, who were now shuffling nervously in their seats. Meanwhile, I moved with deliberate patience, every motion calculated, every step unhurried. This wasn't my first dance, and it wouldn't be my last.

Making my way around to the passenger side, I opened the door with a silent ease. The pain was coming for him, but he was too stupid to know it. He lashed out with a clumsy kick, one last act of defiance. Rookie mistake. Before he could try anything else, I fired a round into his leg.

Boom!

"Arghhh!" he howled, clutching his bleeding leg like it could keep his life from spilling out with his blood. That kind of panic always made people easy to handle. I grabbed him by the collar and dragged him out of the car with ease, dumping him onto the concrete like a sack of garbage.

"Come on, man! I don't know yo' cousin," he screamed. "Fuck! Spare me. Please! I got money. You can have it all. Take it. Just don't kill me."

Kneeling just enough to be face level with him, I stared deep into his eyes, looking past his soul – and finding nothing worth saving. Mercy had no seat at this table. My voice was low, calm, like I was reminding him of an overdue invoice.

"You made a mistake touching my family. That debt you owe? Priceless," I said, my voice as cold as the barrel I pressed to his forehead. He didn't get to beg again. His last expression was a messy blend of terror and regret.

I squeezed the trigger four times.

Boc! Boc! Boc! Boc!

His head snapped back with each slug as his body went limp, nerves firing their last spasms before giving up the fight. The other man in the car – a pathetic soul in the backseat – started screaming the moment he saw his buddy's face erupt. I ignored his cries. They didn't move me.

Instead, I walked back to the car's front seat. Pulling a gas container from the floorboard, I twisted off the cap and began generously dousing the inside of their car, ensuring every corner was primed to burn. Gasoline had an unmistakable smell, one that paired perfectly with death. Satisfied, I tore a strip of fabric from the dead guy's bloodied shirt and stepped away, keeping my movements deliberate. The lighter in my pocket sparked to life with one flick.

I exhaled, steady and slow, like this was therapy for me. Tossing the fabric into the gasoline-soaked interior, I turned away before the flame even caught. The scream started immediately – his voice sharp, shrill, desperate – but I was already walking back, never stopping to watch the fire spread.

The inferno roared behind me, lighting the night in hellish orange, but my work was done. Justice wasn't about fairness. It was about balance. Tonight, the scales tipped in my favor.

Sliding back into the passenger seat of our ride, I glanced at Rude Boy, who was watching me out of the corner of his eye, his face unreadable. Ghost didn't show fear either, but curiosity lingered on both their faces. I didn't bother explaining myself. I just leaned back, relaxed, and reached for the radio. I turned the volume up slightly and let the rhythm of the music replace the screams in my ears.

"You can pull off now," I said, giving him a nod.

Rude Boy tilted his head, acknowledging without question, and the car slowly rolled away from the scene. The fire blazed brightly in the rearview mirror, the black smoke curling upwards into the night sky. I didn't take a last glance. It wasn't personal; it was business. But as the fire faded into the distance, I had the gnawing sense this wasn't over. No, this was just the beginning.

The door had been kicked open, and it wasn't closing anytime soon.

~

Agent Jamiyah's Safe House

"Yes, Pa, capeesh." Zeus ended the phone call with his dad.

Zeus was pushing hard to get them back to New York, making it clear that this wasn't just a casual retreat. He had a reputation to uphold. Zeus was never one to step aside for comfort. He'd always been the one to handle business for the Black Star Mafia, and this time would be no different. For now, he was stuck in Atlanta, waiting on the so-called move Rude Boy had been planning against Taki, the woman who fancied herself dangerous, but Zeus saw her as a problem that needed solving. His men, restless and frustrated, were starting to lose patience. Zeus didn't tolerate failure or waste time, and heading back to New York without a resolution was out of the question.

"I would like to know exactly what we're waiting for with me getting my hands on this bitch. Are we sure this nigga know who he's even looking for or what?"

"Would you just chill, dude? You the one that drove all the way from up top to an area that you unfamiliar with. We can't just jump ourselves in the water because you have a pop-up beef that we didn't know existed. This has to end, and I'm right beside him until this shit blows over. We all still have lives, but if we're gonna jump headfirst into a death match, let's at least do it with some sense." I brushed his negativity off.

"It's easy for you to say, especially since you're a federal agent working alongside killers, expecting your word to be trusted. I don't trust you any further than I can throw you. Let me make this clear; my problem isn't just with one of you. It's with all of you. Sure, maybe I get that you're all pinning this on that woman, throwing her under the bus. But if no one here steps up and takes accountability, then I still have a bone to pick – with every last one of you. Don't make me repeat myself. I don't like having to ask twice."

He wasn't backing down. At least, that was how it felt to me. This guy seemed dead set on butting heads with us, even though he hadn't

85

figured out his own plan. I had to make sure he at least understood where I was coming from. That much was crucial.

Meanwhile, the Italian Mafia was creeping around my neighborhood like they were the Corleone family, running the streets without a care, and it left me uneasy at best. I had no choice but to put up with this traveler's relentless attitude until Rude Boy finally decided to make his move – whatever it was. He was keeping me completely in the dark, saying, "The fewer people who know the plan, the better the chances it succeeds."

It wasn't much to go on, but for now, I had to trust Rude Boy. Still, it didn't make things any easier with everything else going on.

"Believe me, I don't want you here longer than you have to be. If it was my decision, I would throw the dumb bitch in your arms and let you keep her for free."

In the mix of the conversation, Ghost, Rude Boy, and a few new guests stepped through the front door. Zeus immediately stood to his feet to talk, but I cut in before he could.

"So, how do we take this next jump because if we haven't killed this bitch in the next forty-eight hours, we all will be running from the government for the rest of our lives. We haven't even had a decent meal since this shit transpired, and now she might be placing these pieces together kind of quickly," I too was ready to get this shit on the road.

"We've got a lot on our plate," Rude Boy said, his voice low but firm. "But I think this runs deeper than anyone realizes. JoJo just found out where Shanti's been stashed, and I made damn sure he didn't leave his spot. He's not making a move until our end is secured. This is it. It's time to deal with this bitch once and for all." He paused, locking eyes with Zeus. "You're the one who said Yazi was family. I'm riding for him all the way, no questions. Just make sure your team is ready for the storm that's about to hit."

Zeus shifted his gaze from Rude Boy to me then back to Rude Boy again, his arms still folded tightly across his broad chest. The displeasure etched into his face was unmistakable, the stern lines forming a portrait of disapproval. Finally, after a brief but weighted silence, he unfolded his arms, releasing a soft, measured sigh.

His voice, calm yet unyielding, broke through the tension in the air like a blade. "This is what we live for," he said, each word ringing with purpose, leaving no room for uncertainty. His eyes locked onto Rude Boy, the weight of his command sinking deep. "If you'd be so kind, I'd consider it an honor if you'd take the lead," he added, his tone resolute yet tinged with an unexpected layer of respect.

I nodded, stepping closer to him, lowering my voice so the others couldn't hear. Even though everyone knew what was at stake tonight, this part was just between us. "What do you need me to do?"

"I need you to finish things on your end, while I take care of this bitch," he said, his eyes dark with resolve. "JoJo knows his role, and now you've got yours. Don't try to play hero for anyone tonight. Understand? Just lock down that spot behind me. Whatever happens, it's on you to make sure no one gets in after I step into that building. We've got backup from three outer districts, so this might be our only shot to get Shanti and her father back."

I clenched my jaw, his words pressing down on me like a heavy weight. "How can I promise that when I don't even know if you'll make it back out?"

"You can," he said, his tone turning softer, though it didn't lose its edge. "I need you to. I'm tired, Jamiyah. Tired of all this. Knowing my family's safe because of what we did tonight is the only future I can see. It's the only thing worth fighting for now. All the ones who've stood with us, everyone who's gone down for the cause… They deserve to see that future too. There's no debate about this. I've already set people on the lookout for our Fed guy, and if it comes to it, we'll take down the whole damn police force if that's what it takes. But this? This is how it ends."

His words hit me like bricks, their weight filling the air between us. I took a moment, just watching him, as he stood there, resolute but almost… weary. Finally, I nodded, the gravity of the moment anchoring me.

"Alright," I said quietly but firmly. "I promise. I've got it. I swear nobody's getting through once you go in. Just do me one favor, Rude Boy…"

His gaze softened faintly, and I felt the tiniest shift in the tension between us, though it didn't break entirely.

"Promise me you'll try to make it back out. I mean it," I said, my voice tight. "We're not leaving anyone behind. You lead us to this moment – let's walk away from all this together."

Rude Boy gave a subtle nod, his jaw tightening as if to keep himself from saying too much. But the unspoken understanding between us was clear.

This wasn't just another fight. This was *the* fight. One way or another, this would decide everything.

Even though he didn't respond verbally, I knew my words had struck a nerve with this black-hearted man. For the next three hours, we sat down with Zeus' crew, hammering out a plan. Once Rude Boy laid everything on the table, everyone knew their roles and was ready to move on the mission.

"Listen," Rude Boy said, his voice cutting through the tension hanging in the air. "The next time we meet, this needs to be done. We all know what's at stake, so stay sharp, watch your backs, and get out of harm's way."

"Will do," I replied, the weight of his words settling in my chest.

Before I could dwell on the dangers ahead, the sound of tires screeching against asphalt drew my attention. My gaze shot upward to see three black Ford Explorers barreling into the parking lot of my townhome complex. As the vehicles skidded to a stop, the unmistakable blue and red strobe lights flickered in their windshields, and my gut sank. The agency had found us.

Zeus' crew didn't hesitate for a second. They scrambled into their cars, engines roaring as they peeled out like bats out of hell. But before Rude Boy could even think of his next move, the trucks jerked to a halt, and Agent Wilburn stepped out of the driver's seat of the lead vehicle. A handful of burly agents – rednecks through and through – poured out behind him.

"Khalifa Bah," Wilburn barked, venom dripping from his words. "You're under fucking arrest! Your actions have brought terror to this city. Turn around and put your hands on your head!" His hand hovered menacingly over the grip of his sidearm.

Rude Boy turned to look at each of us, but before anyone could blink, Ghost was already pulling his weapon.

Poc! Poc!

Two shots rang out, finding their target in a plainclothes officer's chest. Chaos erupted instantly. Gunfire exploded from the agents' side as everyone scrambled for cover. I ducked low, adrenaline pumping like fire in my veins, as Ghost shielded me with his body. He was relentless, letting off rounds, forcing the agents to retreat just far enough to buy us a sliver of breathing room.

Boc! Boc! Boc! Boc! Boc!

Ghost's shots thundered through the night, shredding the air between us and the agents. The chaotic orchestra of gunfire didn't let up as he maneuvered us toward the opposite side of the street, desperately trying to break through their line. The agents, regrouping quickly, realized we weren't planning on surrendering. They bore down again, their bullets whizzing past us. Two wars – the one in front of us and the one still ahead with Taki — were too much to handle. But we couldn't back down now. We had to finish this.

Rude Boy fired round after round, covering us as best he could. The tension was suffocating. We had no choice but to get Ghost's car. He dove into the driver's seat of his SRT Challenger, turning the key frantically. I stumbled into the passenger seat just as he hit the gas, sending the tires shrieking as the Challenger spun a perfect 360. Gravel kicked up in our wake. Without hesitation, Ghost gunned the engine toward Rude Boy, pulling alongside him. Rude Boy swung the back door open and leapt in, barely pausing as he aimed out the window. His pistol barked again as he focused his fire on Agent Wilburn and his men.

The agents didn't stop. Bullets tore into the night, ricocheting off Ghost's car in metallic screeches. The tires screeched as Ghost floored the gas pedal, the Challenger nearly tipping onto two wheels as it rocketed out of the parking lot. My heart pounded so hard I could feel it in my throat.

"What the hell kind of cops do y'all have up here?" Ghost yelled while keeping his eyes locked on the road ahead. "They shoot first and ask questions later!"

"We're good. We're good," Rude Boy said from the backseat, his voice calm but tense. "Stick to the plan. We can't afford to turn back now."

I leaned back in my seat, my pulse still racing wildly. What had just happened felt like something ripped straight out of a big-budget action movie. Cops blazing down on a team of outlaws, gunfire roaring, tires squealing – except this wasn't fiction and the stakes were as real as the bullets flying past my head. In the back of my mind, I knew that this wouldn't be the end. By sunrise, more blood would be spilled, the body count rising higher. I just prayed it wouldn't include one of us. Time was running out, and we were running out of options.

SHANTI

efeat wasn't the right word for what I felt in that moment. No, it was something much heavier, deeper. Raw pain and blistering anger coursed through my veins in tandem, leaving me shaking. Truthfully, if I'd had a gun in my hand, I would've gladly fought for my life and Dad's, and without hesitation, I would've killed that venomous bitch, Taki. The thought made my stomach churn. After all the horror she orchestrated – my mother's death, the beatings, the endless torment at the hands of her underlings – I wasn't sure I even recognized myself anymore. She had us forcibly removed from Nigeria after my mother's murder, dragging us back to the States in chains like we were nothing.

Yet as much as I ached, my mind was fixated on Khalifa, my soul twisting in uncertainty about what might have become of him. He was out there somewhere, but was he safe? Was he even still alive? The doubts burned a hole in my chest. If Khalifa knew what was happening, I was certain he wouldn't leave me and my father stranded like this. No, something had to be keeping him away. Something big. Something out of his control.

I turned my gaze to my father, slumped on the hard, freezing metal bunk beside me – so different now than the proud and gentle man I'd known all my life. I reached out, rubbing his shoulder softly. "Are you okay?" I asked, my voice low. His silence had been deafening for months, and though I tried to connect with him, each passing day felt like I was losing him more and more.

Dad had barely spoken since my mother's death. The light in his eyes, the infectious humor in his words – all of it had been drained, leaving behind the hollow shell of a man beaten down by grief and captivity. For two months, our world had been reduced to this nightmare – stale jail cell air, crumbling walls that reeked of mildew, and the bare scraps of old snacks we had no choice but to call meals. The sink barely worked, spurting filthy water just good enough to quench our thirst and wipe off the day's grime. Sometimes, I genuinely wondered if we'd been dropped into the set of some post-apocalyptic prison movie, like *Death Race*, trapped in a place where survival meant giving up your soul.

"How did a man like this ever convince you that he had your best interest? Rude Boy, Khalifa, whatever the hell you call him – he promised me he'd protect you," Dad muttered at last, breaking the silence. His voice was hoarse, almost unrecognizable after so many days of stillness. He leaned his back against the wall and shut his eyes, his exhaustion plain to see in the lines around his mouth. "I never wanted to see you get hurt. And now, I feel like I failed you, baby girl. I failed us both."

"Dad." I crouched in front of him, gripping his hands as if by holding him, I'd give him my strength. "Don't you dare say that. None of what's happened is your fault. I know it feels like we're not gonna make it. I know. But we're fighters. We're strong, and you raised me to believe that no matter what, we stick together. Mom wouldn't want anything else for us. She'd want us to believe we could make it out of this."

He frowned, shaking his head. "I just... I don't know, honey. I sure hope you're right. But Rude Boy..." His voice turned bitter when he said the name. "I don't trust him. Maybe he loved you once, but love doesn't mean much when it lets you get taken like this."

I felt a surge of emotion rise, thick and hot in my throat. "Daddy, don't do that please. Rude Boy – he may have his flaws, but he loves me. I know he does. If he knew where we were, he would have found a way to get us by now. That's how much I believe in him. He wouldn't have just left us here – to this." I waved helplessly at the grimy walls around us.

He sighed and shut his eyes again, the tension etched into his features seeming to soften just a bit. "I sure hope you're right... I really do. I'm just glad we're still here together. Family, right?" His lips tilted into a small, flickering smile, one that almost brought tears to my eyes. "That's what it's all about, right? Sticking together. It's not much, but at least I got you, kiddo."

I leaned in and kissed his forehead, a simple act of comfort that I hoped carried the weight of everything I wanted to say. "Yeah, Daddy. We've got each other. God's got us too, and I believe that... No, I know that we're going to be okay."

But as I said the words, the gravity of the situation bore down on me, forcing me to think about how we were going to make it. I hated that he'd been dragged into the middle of this chaos. Hated that his life had to be weighed down by my choices. Still, as much as I hated myself for that, the small flame of hope I carried inside refused to go out. One way or another, we were getting out of this alive. We had to.

～

Taki
District 1

My mind was in overload with trying to enforce my plans, and I was ready to kill everyone and do shit myself, which was always the best way. I had to make a run down to District 1 to set up my final business meeting with the Bentleys. They were the last piece that I needed in order to control the complete drug trafficking operation throughout Atlanta. I carried the biggest port for the marijuana and pills, thanks to Rude Boy, and I was also the biggest cocaine district as of the beginning of my reign. I just needed their button pushed on letting my Kiss Squad operate their business for them, and the rest was history. It was hard to stop a bitch that had her hands in every play imaginable.

Pulling up to Club Cheetah, I parked my car and used my spare keys to get access through the back entrance. I strolled my way to the office and headed straight for the safe. It didn't take too long to enter the combination and grab what I needed. After snatching up my business papers and four hundred thousand in cash, I placed a call to Vince but didn't receive an answer.

My mind said that something smelled fishy, but I just didn't catch it quick enough. By the time I exited the office, I looked up into eyes of the nasty agent bitch pointing her gun directly at me.

"Don't even think about it, Taki. We've been chasing you for too long, and this shit isn't going on any longer. Now, put your hands up and don't make me shoot you because I will," she threatened with her hand steady on the trigger.

I smirked evilly, glaring into her eyes. I could see that she feared me. I smelled it. She was weak and had obviously been blinded by Rude Boy's dick like us all. I wouldn't let her beat me even if she had the win right in her palms.

I raised my hands in surrender.

"Ain't it crazy how you out here chasing me and you still ain't accomplished whatever it was you were doing? I'm not your priority, sweetie. You're fighting a war that you have nothing to do with, and you're gonna lose. Did Rude Boy tell you that you were bait to get his girl, Shanti, back?" I asked, watching her face shrivel up like a prune.

"Forget what you're saying. I don't care what Rude Boy has on his agenda because I know what's on mines, and you're the reason for all my headache. This isn't about Rude, you stupid cunt. This is for my partner, Agent Lace," she spat, raising the gun toward me.

I rushed toward her and dived, tackling her to the ground. I took a small blow to the head from her trying to stop me, but I was all gas on the pedal to make it out. Once I saw the gun slide from her hands, I stood up and tossed my guard in the air. She jumped to her feet, and before she could think about rushing for it, we were locked up, swinging blow for blow. I didn't have any intention of letting this ho beat me, and she wasn't going down easy. We held on to each other and traded fists until she tripped up on her heel and fell.

Landing on top of her, I placed two more punches on her face and rushed for the door. I scooped up her gun and didn't hesitate to shoot a few times behind me in case she thought to put up a chase.

Boc! Boc! Boc!

I didn't even think to look behind me, and my mind was set that the next time I saw this bitch, she was going to die on the spot. I was down bad without my security, and I couldn't allow this deal to blow over with the Bentleys. It'd cause everything to fall.

Scrambling out the back door of the club, I quickly made my way to my car and jumped inside. By the time I was starting the engine and pulling out, the agent was running into the driveway at full speed, as if she was going to match the speed of my car. I pushed the pedal on my Mercedes Benz and left that stupid bitch in the wind.

My phone ringing in my pocket snapped my adrenaline down to normal. I took a small breath and answered.

"This is Taki."

"Glad I was able to catch you, Taki. You know who, of course. I was calling you about our proposal and meeting that's set for us today. It has come to my attention that you have made bad beds with people I have good ties and blood with, and I'm afraid that's bad for business. See, Taki, in this game, we respect each other, and once the respect is gone, there is no need to discuss money, understanding, or business because the focus has already been thrown out the window. As far as our product and connection, you're stripped of access, and you can remove any workers you have harboring our locations by tonight. So sorry this had to come on short notice, but you do understand that I am about business."

"You do understand that I'm the wrong one to back out on, Mr. Bentley. I respect you for sure. You have power and money to scare most, but I'm a renegade with nothing to lose but life, so I'll tell you this as nicely as possible. For your betrayal, I'll be sure to slaughter your entire family in your face the first chance I get, and you better believe I keep promises," I snapped into the phone before tossing it into my backseat.

I had to get Vince and the rest of my Kiss Squad crew ready because if crashing out was meant, we were gonna wreck everything moving. That was guaranteed.

~

JoJo
District 1

I'd been waiting outside the condominium complex on Midtown Street for the past four hours, watching ever individual that I saw pass through. My eyes were on the lookout for Taki, but I still had yet to spot her. Up the street, I watched as a few of her associates from the Kiss Squad moved in and out of the old precinct as if it were the new hangout for the hood. Beside it was a row of commercial businesses, and across the street, going down, was the same. That was District 1 for you. All work, no play. I had intel that Shanti was inside the precinct, and when the coast was clear, I finally made my move, stepping out of the car.

I'd dressed in some simple Armani slacks and a collared shirt. I wore a grey wig that made me resemble an old man, and a tight fitted Chicago Bears hat hugged my head. I walked slowly up the empty precinct stairs and walked inside. The first officer at the metal detector gazed up at me for a second, but when his eyes reached mine again, my gun was raised up toward his face, pulling the trigger

Boom!

Moving past the machines, I could hear the walkie talkie in the back go off, and two more officers came from the back, yelling.

"Freeze!"

I fired three shots, hitting the first one in the head.

Boom! Boom! Boom!

He dropped to the floor, but the blast from a shotgun the second officer held forced me to collapse.

Boom!

It felt like my head exploded, and my gun was resting on the floor a few feet away from me. I noticed the officer cock the shotgun back a second time, and I immediately flew for my pistol. By the time I reached it, I landed on my back and rolled over, letting go another four shots quickly.

Poc! Poc! Poc! Poc!

96

All four found home into his chest, forcing him to fire a shot into the ceiling.

I gathered myself and aimed my pistol in front of me as I continued toward the back. I was surprised the building was so empty. I knew it was run by crooked enforcement and, of course, Taki.

Crossing the double doors, the hairs on my neck stood up, and I felt someone near me. I didn't waste a moment turning around, giving them the last few bullets in my gun.

Poc! Poc! Poc!

The huge guard hunched over and nearly fell on top of me. I pushed his body over and took a second to look around. There was a line of empty cells and one office desk that held a ton of office papers. I moved down the row of cells until I spotted Shanti and her father balled up on the bottom bunk.

"Shanti!"

"Oh. my God, JoJo. How did you find us? Where is Rude Boy?" She instantly went into a panic.

"I can't explain right now. It's a lot, but I have to get you both somewhere safe and far away from here."

"What about Rude Boy?" she asked me as I popped the lock to the cell door, opening it up.

"Rude Boy asked me to make sure you all are safe. He wants to handle this on his own, so you know I couldn't go against that. I have to get you out of here," I repeated and helped them both to their feet.

Making our way back to the front of the precinct, Shanti looked me in the eyes.

"Is he coming back?"

"I don't know, Shanti. I honestly don't."

Walking out of the building, I tried to make our way to the car as discreetly as possible. Once I got them both in safely, I hit the pedal out of the parking lot and dialed Rude's number on my phone.

∾

Agent Jamiyah Porter
Rude Boy's Mansion

After we placed a night of networking around this dumb ass city, Rude Boy paused us in District 7 at his main residence. Since the war with Taki had spread, he started to rest his head on the outskirts to be one step ahead of all his enemies. His home was beautiful. It was decked out from the flat screen televisions to the furniture. I noticed a lot of Jamaican and African art, which was something I never noticed in any man's home. It was a surprise to see his taste.

He allowed us to make ourselves at home. After we discussed our plans for how we would fall out tomorrow, the hours started to pass, and sitting in the guest room alone forced me to think of what could be on Rude Boy's mind at this moment besides Shanti.

Climbing out of the bed I was resting in, I slid in my Louis Vuitton flip-flops and headed down the hallway to his master bedroom. I knocked twice but didn't receive an answer. Placing my ear up to the door, I knocked again before turning the knob.

I noticed the lights off, and I slowly crept in. I could hear the sound of his shower running heavily as if the door was open. A sliver of light shined from the cracked bathroom door and illuminated my skin, and the immediate thought of how this man looked danced through my mind. I was at a loss for words when it came to him, and that was my only problem. I didn't know why.

The room was silent as I crept toward the door, my flip flops brushing lightly across the carpet. My breath was shallow, my heartbeat loud in my ears, but the tantalizing thought of him spurred me forward. With trembling fingers, I reached for the handle, my hand hovering for a moment as if to give myself one last chance to rethink this. But I didn't stop. I couldn't. Slowly, I turned the knob, easing the door open, careful to avoid the creak of its hinges as I peeked inside.

The bathroom was dimly lit, steam curling and clinging to the air as if the walls were breathing with heat. Then there he was, standing under the rush of the showerhead, his body glistening under the cascade of water. My eyes traced every sharp line and curve of his muscular back before drifting lower. He reached up, his hand sliding through his wet hair, and it was like he was carved by some divine hand, intentional in every detail.

I froze in place, mesmerized, hunger curling in the pit of my stomach. An ache pulsed between my thighs, my fingers brushing there instinctively, just the lightest touch; and still, it sparked fire. My lips parted, a shaky breath escaping. I tried to quiet the swirl of thoughts that raced in my head, my imagination painting a wild picture of him stepping toward me, grasping my body with the same strength I saw in his every movement.

For a moment, I let myself get lost in the fantasy, my lids falling half-shut as I pictured his hands pressing into my skin, his breath hot against my neck. But then, as if the pull of my thoughts somehow beckoned him, he turned.

His head shifted first then the chiseled curve of his shoulders. His eyes locked on mine, catching me frozen in the doorway. Time seemed to stop. I couldn't move, couldn't think – as if his stare alone had rooted me to the ground. His expression wasn't surprised though; it was intense – dark – like he wasn't sure whether to call me out for the intrusion or to give in to some unspoken force pulling us together.

The water shut off, the sound of the stream coming to a sudden halt, as the room seemed to fall completely still. My heart thundered in my chest when he took a step forward. Droplets of water clung to his body, trailing rivulets down the hard lines of his chest, his abdomen. My throat felt dry. He didn't stop to grab a towel. He didn't even hesitate as he closed the space between us, standing tall and imposing as he stared down at me.

"This is an awkward place to always meet up," he said, his voice low, words tinged with amusement.

I swallowed hard, trying to focus on anything other than the overwhelming heat radiating from his freshly showered skin. "Sometimes it just happens," I murmured, barely aware that I was even capable of forming words.

His lips tilted into the faintest smirk, and then suddenly, his hand encircled my wrist. His touch was firm, guiding, but not demanding. Still, I followed him without question as he moved us into the bedroom. The steam from the bathroom followed us, lingering like a witness.

In one swift motion, his hands found the hem of my shirt, lifting it over my head. My breath hitched as the cool air grazed my bare skin, and before I could second-guess anything, I felt my shorts slipping down my hips, pooling at my feet. I stepped out of them almost instinctively, standing exposed before him. His dark gaze traveled over me, real and unrelenting in its weight.

"You're beautiful," he whispered like it was some vow.

My chest rose and fell sharply as he took my hand again, leading me toward the bed. His palm rested at the small of my back as he lowered me onto it, his fingers effortlessly gliding along my thigh, his touch like a slow tease. The warmth of his breath traced my skin, and then his lips followed, trailing kisses that sent sparks firing along my nerves.

When his mouth finally found the center of my heat, I gasped, my back arching upward. His tongue moved with an intoxicating rhythm, firm and deliberate as it danced over my clit. My hands dug into the sheets, clutching tightly as sharp waves of pleasure rolled over me.

"Uhn…" I moaned, my hand slipping to the back of his head, my fingers tangling in his hair. I wanted to push him deeper, closer, to beg him never to stop. His groan of satisfaction vibrated against me, and it only fueled the blaze he was building. It felt like he was pulling me apart and putting me back together all at once, his mouth working with precision that made me tremble.

As I was nearing the edge, he lifted his head abruptly, leaving me panting and aching for more. I barely had a moment to register his movements before he guided me onto all fours, pulling me gently by the hips. He positioned me at the edge of the bed, my knees pressing into the mattress as he stood behind me.

He ran his hands over the curve of my ass, gripping it firmly. Then, with a sharp smack, his palm connected with my skin, leaving behind a sharp sting that dissolved into warmth. I gasped, but before I could recover, he pressed into me.

His length filled me completely, eliciting a cry that I couldn't stop even if I wanted to. "Ahh!" I heard myself, my body responding before my mind could catch up, surrendering fully to him.

He moved with a deliberate pace at first – slow, testing, letting me feel every inch of him before pulling back and diving again, deeper this time. His grip tightened on my hips, his rhythm intensifying, as he lost himself in me. Every thrust sent a jolt through me, leaving me unable to think of anything beyond the sensation of him stretching and claiming me.

The sound of skin meeting skin, heavy breathing, and muffled moans filled the room as the two of us fell into a rhythm that felt primal, raw. It wasn't just lust; it was hunger, undeniable and unrelenting, and it threatened to consume us both. His thrusts grew deeper, harder, and relentless, and I could feel every inch of him inside me, pressing and stretching until the pressure settled low in my belly. Each time he buried himself to the hilt, the force rocked me forward, as though he was trying to make sure I felt all of him. His hands gripped my hips with a fierce possessiveness, using them to pull me back into each intense thrust. The sound of our bodies colliding was loud and intimate, filling the space around us with the heat of our shared intensity.

My fingers clawed at the sheets, desperate for something sturdy to hold, as it felt like my body was on the verge of losing control. "Oh, my God," I whimpered, the tension coiling tight in my core as his pace quickened. Beads of sweat formed along my spine, and the heat of his chest hovered closer as he leaned in, his large hands gliding up to cup my breasts.

His fingers pinched and rolled my nipples, a fresh wave of intensity shooting through me. "You feel so damn good," he growled, his voice low and hoarse with desire. The sound of it sent a shiver across my skin, and I arched my back instinctually, pressing myself harder into him.

My heartbeat was erratic, drumming in my ears, as my stomach flipped and clenched, a sure sign that I was on the verge of release. "I... Ahh, I can't," I gasped, the words breaking apart as my body could no longer hold back the wave that had been building deep within me. All at once, my release rushed through me, sharp and intoxicating, hitting every nerve like lightning.

My body trembled under him as my orgasm coursed through me, my muscles tensing and pulsing around him. "Ohhhh!" I cried out, my moan breaking into a small scream as my eyes rolled shut, the intensity washing over me in a blinding rush.

He wasn't finished. I could feel it – the way his breath quickened, the way his grip on me tightened. "Damn," he muttered under his breath, still moving, his focus unrelenting. Even as I trembled with the aftershocks of my release, he continued chasing his own pleasure, driving harder into me. The rhythm was desperate now, driven by pure need, and I found myself grinding backward to meet him.

The wet sound of him sliding in and out of me filled the room, paired with our heavy breathing and the occasional smack of his hand against my ass. "That's it," he groaned, his voice thick with pleasure, as I started to bounce against him, rolling my hips faster. He grabbed a firm hold of my waist, guiding me, our movements perfectly synced as if our bodies knew exactly how to ignite one another.

Even though it wasn't supposed to happen like this tonight, even if it wasn't planned, the way he felt in me – the way I craved him – was undeniable. The thought buzzed quietly in my mind, but the sensations he pulled from me drowned out everything else.

He finally tensed behind me, pulling my hips flush against his, as he grunted deeply and spilled into me, his release hot and claiming. I could feel every pulse and shudder of his body as he released completely, using the connection between us to draw out the last of his pleasure. His hand slid along my back, a soft caress now compared to his earlier roughness.

For several long moments, we remained tangled and trembling, breaths heavy as we both began to come down from the high. Finally, his hands left my waist, and he collapsed onto the bed beside me, dragging me down with him. We lay there, a tangled mess of bodies, legs entwined, as the night air cooled the sweat on our skin.

The silence was thick but not entirely uncomfortable. I turned my face toward him, and as I did, I caught the slight flicker of hesitation in his dark eyes. He stared up toward the ceiling, and for the first time tonight, the weight of guilt seemed to settle over him. It showed in the way his brows drew together, the way his lips pressed tightly into a thin line.

Rude Boy ran a hand over his face, exhaling a sharp breath. "This wasn't supposed to happen," he murmured, almost to himself, his voice suddenly softer now – conflicted.

I propped myself up on my elbow, studying his expression. It was clear that his mind had shifted. He was no longer just here in this moment with me. No, part of him – maybe all of him – was thinking about her. Shanti. And I wasn't foolish enough to ignore it. I could practically feel her presence between us, even though she wasn't here.

"I know..." My voice was quiet, barely more than a whisper. There was a weight in my chest, but at the same time, there was an odd relief in understanding. "You don't have to explain."

He turned his head toward me then, his gaze softening, as his dark eyes held regret – and something else. Gratitude, maybe. For the comfort I'd given him tonight, even if it hadn't been mine to give.

"I don't want you to think you're just... this," he said, his fingers tentatively brushing along my arm. It was hard for him to explain, and I could see the strain laced in his features.

"I don't," I reassured him, my voice steady, as if to ease his turmoil. "And I'm not sure tonight was about that anyway."

He nodded, but the silence spoke volumes. We both knew what this was, what lines had been crossed. All the heat, the passion, the way we'd lost ourselves in each other – it wouldn't change where he belonged. And it wasn't with me.

We lay there quietly for a while, neither of us willing to move, stretching the moment just a little longer, before the reality of everything caught up. Even though I didn't know how any of this would settle tomorrow, tonight, the facts were simple.

He needed something. And for one night, I gave it to him. "I know what's on your mind without even asking," I said, tapping on his chest before sitting up beside him.

He looked over at me in confusion.

"What makes you so sure of that?"

"Because you're only compassionate about a few things, and I've found them out in the little time I've been around you. Family, friends, and business. It's cold to live in a world like that where you have no freedom for the things you love doing instead of things you have to. You're a great man. I see that in you every time I look at you. I want to see this work out in your favor. I just don't want you to be so hard on yourself while we try and make it happen."

He nodded before speaking.

"I appreciate your kind words because I've never had them offered before. I'm like this for numerous reasons, but this is why I've lasted so long. My family is all I got. Loyalty is everything. It's funny you see the good in me, and you're a cop." He smirked.

"No, what's funny is you don't see the good in yourself. Rude Boy, you are a leader, but you are not meant to be the leader of Atlanta. You're meant to be more. Get Shanti back and start over. In my opinion, leave the country. It's worth a shot." I gave him my honest opinion.

He pondered on my response for a second and rubbed my back softly.

"Thank you, forreal."

"Anytime."

I climbed out of his bed, wrapping his bedroom sheet around my body.

"I guess I'll be seeing you in the morning, sir. I have to shower and think of how I can cry myself a life." I smiled, walking out.

Even though I tried to mask my feelings, I truly felt for that man in the wildest ways ever. It had to be roots because he wasn't even applying effort. I didn't know if he would succeed at getting Shanti back, but I was going to stand beside him until he got the answer.

RUDE BOY

Club Foreign

Sliding down to District 8, I gained insight on a few whereabouts of where this nigga, Vince, and Taki's Kiss Squad crew posted at. Club Foreign was always the biggest to everyone's knowledge. It was controlled mainly by the Asians from Doraville. They were highly powerful around the country, of course, but they rarely allowed access in their business. Instead, they bought the business and allowed the faces to be the so-called bosses. In return, they kicked out for all transport, events, parties, or drugs that crossed through that club. It was a bigger table than just the head of Atlanta. The Mafia was another thing, which was why I understood when Zeus made his presence known. It was business and had to be done. I needed to know if these clowns were working out of Yung's spot because, if so, one of them would tell me what I needed, or the establishment would have to close for a while.

Ghost checked his gun before we entered, and I gave him the look that whatever happened, we came first. We entered the building and maneuvered through the guests inside. People were sitting at tables, having meals, and the floor was packed with live civilians from across the entire state. We both slid past the fun and moved toward the small steps that led up to the VIP. My eyes instantly landed on Vince and a few more Kiss Squad members. Yung had his back turned, dressed in a Gucci suit, with a phone to his ear. Me and Ghost crossed the space between us, and I tapped his shoulder lightly.

"What the fuck, Rude Boy? What a surprise. What can I get ya to drink?" He held open his arms.

"Uh, nothing at the moment, Yung, but I do need a quick chat for ya that can't wait. Those pussies right there, they work for Taki. Turns out she has my girl, and there's bad blood on my end of these streets, and these clowns know where to find her." I pointed at Vince.

He slowly approached with three Kiss Squad members at his side as if they were ready to start some fuckery. I could see the scariness in his eyes. I knew that he just wanted to save face.

"Looks like you got a problem with us or some'n, nigga. We already told you. This city is ours. We can debate, we can argue, but we damn sure ain't about to lie. Y'all fools must be lost," he ranted with hostility

"Wait, hold the fuck up. We can't do this here, Rude. I lost my place behind this shit before. Let's talk."

"Yeah, let's talk." I pulled out my Glock 17 and started to pull the trigger.

Boc! Boc! Boc! Boc!

They all quickly took cover, and Ghost fell directly in line and started to fire his pistol. Yung jumped out of our way and dispersed through the building with the rest of the people that were running to the exit.

The Kiss Squad members started to return fire, and I wasted no time. Gunning directly for them, I landed two shots in the first thug's chest, sending him over the glass VIP table.

Boc! Boc!

Shit was flying everywhere, and I could hear the bullets whizzing past my ear as I tried to kill everybody standing next to them. Vince shot his gun recklessly, but he stumbled and moved around until he reached the front exit.

I aimed my gun, firing shots after shot, until he was no longer in my vision.

Boc! Boc! Boc! Boc! Boc!

"Damn it!" I smacked my fist across the wall in anger.

"We gotta go. If that nigga almost got caught once, he can get caught again. These people don't know what to expect right now, Rude Boy. You gotta be a thinker. We'll catch him real soon. Trust me," Ghost assured me as we jogged out the front door.

Getting to the parking lot, we reached the car and jumped inside. Starting the engine, we hightailed out into the streets and mashed the gas toward District 8, heading from their border.

"Taki doesn't have too many more options. She has run out of shit to pull, and I smell us closing in on this bitch. This will be the last stand I can make to save my people. It is what it is." I looked at Ghost, prepared for what was to come.

"Now you talking like we bout to take care of business." He sat back and started to reload his gun.

I had the bitch right where I needed, and I intended on using my advantage wisely.

Taki

I hadn't been down in District 1 for more than an hour when the call came through. Vince had failed. The little white boy, JoJo, had escaped, and he didn't go alone. Shanti and her father were with him, slipping out like shadows in the night. Fury rose in me like fire, and it took everything I had not to throw the phone across the room. Instead, I slammed my hand on the table with enough force to rattle the glass, seething as I tried to think. Where the hell was the rest of my backup? How could they have let this happen?

A few minutes later, my second-in-command messaged me. Our guest was pulling into the driveway. Perfect timing.

It didn't take long before the man stormed into the room, his anger as hot as mine. But his anger wasn't directed at Vince or his failures. No, it was all for me. His nostrils flared as his words came out sharp and accusatory.

"What the hell is going on, Taki? Where's my son, JoJo? I haven't heard a single word about him. Not a thing." His voice was that of a man used to demanding answers – and getting them.

But I didn't flinch. I didn't cower. I didn't back down. Instead, I gave him a cold, sharp smile and met his fury with mine, louder and sharper and infinitely more dangerous.

"You're worried about your son?" I asked, venom dripping from my words. "That boy might not even make it through the next hour. I don't take kindly to little bastards trying to cross me, and your son is a potential enemy. Maybe you forgot who you're talking to. I don't do opposition."

His face twisted in rage, and when he spoke again, his voice was low but steady – a deadly calm. "You must have forgotten I run Atlanta. Everything you've built – you think you're untouchable?" He laughed bitterly, shaking his head. "I'm the reason you have all this. I gave you resources, leverage, power. I built you. I can end you just as quickly. My men can handle my dirty work just fine. Our deal? It's over. We're done here. Get out."

He waved his hand dismissively, and his two guards stepped forward, a silent threat etched on their faces.

Big mistake.

This wasn't his city anymore; it was mine. I wasn't going to let him lecture me in what was now my kingdom, not while I stood at its throne. Anger surged through me like a lightning strike. A cold smile crept across my face as I reached for my gun.

Boom!

Boom!

The two guards didn't even have time to react. Clean shots to the head dropped them where they stood. A deep, hollow silence filled the room, broken only by the echo of the gunshots. Blood pooled beneath their lifeless bodies, spilling like dark ink onto the floor.

The senator froze in place, his arrogance dissolving into terror. He stumbled backward, his chest heaving with panicked breaths. The color drained from his face as he stared at me, his eyes wide.

"You... You can't do this to me, Taki!" His voice cracked, his words trembling.

I let out a laugh – low, dark, and cutting – as I tilted my head at him. All his power, his arrogance, his status – it meant nothing now. Not to me.

"Oh, I can do a hell of a lot more," I said coldly, the muzzle of my gun hovering inches from his face. "Killing is simple. Don't you remember?"

I didn't wait for an answer.

Boom!

The bullet ripped through his skull, silencing him forever. He slumped to the ground slowly, like a puppet whose strings were cut, his blood joining that of his two guards. I stared down at him for a moment, unfazed by the mess. Atlanta had gone to hell long before anyone cared to notice. But unlike the rest of these fools, I wasn't going down with it. This city wouldn't bury me; it would be the foundation I built on. And anyone who thought otherwise would meet the same fate as the senator.

If Rude Boy wanted to start a war over Shanti, I was more than ready to give him one. But first, I had to deal with the ones banging at my door.

The sound of gunfire erupted outside, tearing through the brief silence like thunder. I strolled to the window and saw the chaos unfolding below. My team was locked in a standoff with a crowd of armed men, a scene straight out of an action movie. The air was thick with tension and lead. It was clear that this wasn't going to resolve itself any other way.

Calmly, I checked the chamber of my gun, loading it with practiced ease, before turning my attention to the door. The chaos beyond it called to me like a challenge. If this was my last stand, so be it. I'd go out on my terms.

I tightened my grip on my weapon and stepped forward, ready to meet the action head-on. Death might have been waiting for me on the other side, but I never feared it. Instead, I welcomed it with a sly grin.

And if I was meant to take my last breath tonight, so be it. There would be a hell of a lot more taken before mine.

～

Rude Boy
District 1

My mind was racing, but it wasn't from nerves. I had built my entire life around the principle of taking care of those I loved, and in that moment, I knew I was making the right decision to put everything on the line for my woman. This wasn't a choice I made lightly; it was something deeper, a raw determination to ensure her safety and our future, no matter the cost.

Behind us, a handful of crew members from the outer districts trailed in their vehicles, ready to back us up. This wasn't a sanctioned operation; the senator hadn't approved it, and honestly, we didn't care. Chaos City Day, the day the lines of law and order blurred into oblivion, was no longer just some distant threat. It was our new reality. Everything we had fought for up until this point led us here, to the precipice of a storm we were now forced to embrace head-on.

As Ghost maneuvered the car down Midtown Street, the horizon twisted into something out of a warzone. Ahead, a barricade of trucks and debris blocked the road, and figures with tense postures moved to test the invisible boundaries. My gut tightened because I knew what this meant before it even happened. All hell broke loose in the blink of an eye.

Gunfire erupted, sharp and deafening, cutting through the humid Atlanta air like shards of glass. Ghost cursed under his breath, slamming the brakes and swerving the car to the side of the street. There was no hesitation. The crew vehicles behind us came to a halt, and within moments, our people were spilling out onto the pavement, weapons drawn, joining the chaos erupting in the heart of Downtown Atlanta.

It was surreal – a vicious symphony of shouting, bullet casings hitting concrete, and the acrid stench of gunpowder filling the air. The once-bustling streets of downtown had morphed into a battlefield. This wasn't just another fight; this was war, a turning point that would define everything. And as I gripped my weapon and prepared to step out into the fray, I knew this moment wasn't just about survival. It was about purpose. About her. About us.

"Move! Move!" I yelled as I jumped out of the car, firing shots without hesitation. Adrenaline surged through me; every sound, every movement, seemed amplified. People scattered in every direction, some screaming, others darting behind cover as if the chaos on the streets suddenly wasn't their fight. My pulse quickened as my eyes locked onto Agent Wilburn. He had leapt from his Tahoe, an assault rifle in hand, moving with purpose. The instant he saw me, his gaze narrowed, and without hesitation, he lifted his weapon.

Time slowed for a fraction of a second. There was no doubt about what he was going to do. Before I could raise my gun, the sharp, thunderous sound of gunfire cracked.

Boc! Boc! Boc!

Ghost fired three rounds, drawing Wilburn's attention just long enough to shove me toward the entrance of the condominium complex.

"Go! Now!" Ghost barked, pushing hard on my back.

I didn't waste a second. My feet hit the pavement, and I bolted toward the glass double doors of the building. Gunfire erupted behind me, bullets tearing through the air as I dove headfirst into the lobby, the echo of the shots chasing me inside. My shoulder hit the cold tile, but I scrambled to my feet as quickly as I had dropped. Raising my gun, I scanned the room with precision honed by countless moments like this. Civilians cowered against the walls, their faces pale with fear, some frozen, some trembling as chaos ripped through their city. I didn't blame them.

Jogging toward the elevator at the center of the lobby, my mind raced. My hand shot out to press the call button when a thought struck me, that nagging voice in the back of my head telling me it wasn't safe to wait. My eyes darted to the stairwell on my right, and I knew what I had to do. I veered toward the stairs, taking them three steps at a time, every muscle in my legs burning with the effort. It didn't matter. I couldn't waste time – not even a second.

By the time I reached the tenth floor, I was breathless. Sweat slid down my temple as I shoved open the heavy exit door leading into the hallway. My heart dropped the moment I saw her – Taki – stepping toward the waiting elevator. My weapon was drawn before I even realized it, my training kicking in.

"I never thought I'd see the day I'd have to face you on the other side of the battlefield," I said, my voice tense as I aimed the gun at her back.

She didn't flinch. Instead, she spun around, her pistol already in hand, as if she had been waiting for this moment, expecting it all along. Her expression wasn't one of surprise or fear; it was venomous, her lips curling into a scowl that matched the fire in her eyes.

"No," she said, her voice low but filled with rage that sent a chill through me. "You idiot. You don't even get what this is about. After everything I risked for you. After everything I gave for you. I slaved for you – as your assistant, your so-called friend, your goddamn worker – all to prove my worth. I bent over backward to make you see the value of what I brought to the table. And you…" She shook her head, her voice rising, bitter with fury. "You took it all for granted. You saw me as nothing more than a doormat."

Her grip tightened on the pistol, but she didn't fire. Not yet.

"You didn't value me. Not what I sacrificed. Not what I built. Nothing! And now, I'm tearing it all down!" Her words crackled with rage, and for a moment, standing there with my gun on her, I couldn't tell if she wanted me dead or if she wanted me to understand the depth of her pain.

But a part of me knew. It was both.

"Taki, you've always been my friend. My *fucking* friend," I said, my voice raw with frustration. "You *knew* I loved Shanti. You knew what she meant to me, and still, you tried to take that from me – for your own fantasy, for whatever dream world you thought we could exist in. You're wrong, Taki. You've been wrong this whole time, and I'm putting a stop to it. Today."

My grip on the gun tightened as we locked eyes. Despite my words, a sliver of me hoped she could see the truth in them, that this conversation could end without blood. "You can still walk away," I added, my voice softening just slightly. "It's over. You've already lost."

But I knew, deep down, I wasn't going to let her walk away – not this time. She had caused too much destruction, too much pain. People I cared about had suffered because of her actions, and the path she had chosen couldn't be undone. This wasn't going to end with one of us walking away. Not now.

Taki's expression twisted into something dark, venomous. "No," she said, her voice sharp and laced with rage. "You can either love me, Rude Boy, or you can *bleed* in harmony with that bitch of yours, Shanti."

She leveled her pistol at me, the barrel gleaming under the dim hallway light. I tensed, steadying my aim, while my heart thundered in my chest.

"This doesn't have to go down like this. Just put the gun down, Taki," I said, lowering my tone in an attempt to calm her. "Walk away. Please. You don't have to do this."

Her hand trembled for a brief moment, and I held my breath, watching her wrestle with the shards of anger and pain inside her. But then, she fidgeted in fury, her jaw tight, as her grip steadied once more. Her eyes burned with something wild, something desperate, and I saw the decision before she made it.

"Taki, don't!" I yelled, but it was too late.

The deafening crack of her gunshot filled the hallway, ripping through the tension. Before I had time to think, my instincts took over, and I pulled the trigger.

Boom!

Boc!

The exchange lasted less than a second, but everything slowed down as I watched her stagger back. Taki's body crumpled to the floor, her hands clamped around her neck as blood spilled through her fingers in thick, dark streams. She writhed, her mouth opening and closing as if she were trying to speak, but the only sound that came out was a wet, choking gasp.

I froze, my gun still raised, my breath shallow. "Fuck," I muttered under my breath as I tried to regain control of the moment. That was when I felt it – a deep, searing pain along my side. My hand instinctively dropped to my shirt, and as I pulled it back up, I saw my fingers coated in red. The lower half of my shirt was soaked, and the realization of what had happened hit me like a freight train.

Taki's strangled breaths pulled my focus back to her. She was still alive – barely. Her face twisted in anguish, her breaths ragged, but her eyes stayed locked on me. She was mumbling something, her voice soft and broken. Maybe she was trying to explain herself. Maybe she was begging. Maybe it didn't matter.

Through a sharp burst of pain in my chest, I forced myself to step closer to her, my knees shaking with every movement. The world blurred for a moment as dizziness washed over me, but I fought to stay upright. I couldn't collapse yet. Not yet. Looking down at her with no sympathy, no pity, and no forgiveness, I spoke the words I knew she'd carry to her grave – the words she deserved to hear.

"I told you to walk away," I said coldly, gripping my gun tighter. "Now, you have to kiss your own consequences, bitch."

I raised the weapon again, but my vision swam. My breathing became shallow as my body fought to keep me standing. Still, I locked onto her one last time, determined to end it. With the last shred of my strength, I steadied my aim and pulled the trigger.

Boc!

The shot rang out like thunder against the silence of the hall. I watched the life drain from her eyes as blood pooled beneath her, staining the floor a deep crimson. Her body went still – her last breath vanishing into the air.

It was over.

But my victory felt hollow. My body was giving out on me, the loss of blood pulling the strength from my limbs. The pain surged again, sharper this time, and I knew I didn't have long. Staggering back, I turned to find the nearest exit. Every step felt heavier, the world darkening at the edges of my vision. All I could think about was Shanti – her face, her touch, her voice. She was my anchor, my reason for surviving. I wanted to leave this city, to start over with her, far away from this chaos. I couldn't let Atlanta destroy me.

I made it a few more steps, my knees trembling under the weight of my body. The hallway seemed endless now. I pushed forward until the strength left me, and I collapsed to my knees. My hands hit the cold floor as blackness crept over me. With one final thought of Shanti, a faint prayer that I'd somehow make it back to her, my vision faded completely, and everything went dark.

EPILOGUE

Two Weeks Later
Agent Jamiyah Porter

It had been a few weeks since we lost Rude Boy, and I had to admit, it felt like one of the most gut-wrenching things I'd ever experienced. We weren't exactly close, but there was something about him – an unspoken bond we shared – that stuck with me. Even now, the thought of him was like a shadow I couldn't shake. I didn't need much time to figure out why. Rude Boy had this way of connecting with people, even if it wasn't obvious at first. That connection stayed with you, even after he was gone.

We had barely escaped Agent Wilburn and the Kiss Squad affiliates. It was closer than I wanted to remember. They had us cornered, but with the help of those outer districts – and Ghost's timely intervention before his sudden departure to the Virgin Islands – we managed to make it out of that chaos alive. It was a small miracle, though nothing could shake the sting of losing Rude Boy. Even with the victory, his loss left a hollow feeling in its wake, like we'd lost more than we gained that day.

Stopping at Lincoln Cemetery, JoJo and I got out of the car and started the slow walk toward Rude Boy's burial site. The early afternoon was quiet, and the crisp air carried a stillness that matched the somberness of the day. The crunch of gravel under our feet was the only sound as we moved toward the rows of tombstones. I didn't know what I expected to find, but I certainly didn't expect what I saw as we got closer.

There, standing alone at his grave, was Shanti. She was still as a statue, her arms crossed tightly against her body, her eyes locked on the weathered tombstone as if searching for something it could never give her. Her presence caught me by surprise, though maybe it shouldn't have. If anyone had just as deep a connection to Rude Boy as I did – even deeper, really – it was Shanti. She had her reasons for being here, just like I had mine.

As we approached, I slowed my pace, letting JoJo walk ahead, while I took a deep breath and slid my hands into my jacket pockets. The closer I got to her, the more I could make out how tense she looked, her shoulders rigid and her head slightly bowed. I didn't want to startle her, so I stepped forward cautiously. When I was finally close enough, I stopped a few feet behind her and hesitated for a moment.

"Doesn't seem real, huh?" I said softly, my voice low enough to respect the weight of her grief. It wasn't much, but I hoped it was enough to let her know I was there.

She turned to look at me, tears streaked across her face, her eyes red and swollen. There was a kind of raw pain in her expression that words couldn't capture.

"This is something I'll never get over," she choked out, her voice heavy with sorrow. "He was my best friend. Feeling alone – feeling lost – isn't just a statement anymore. It's my reality now. I have to start all over."

I stayed silent, giving her space to release her pain. Her words tore into me, but I knew this wasn't about me. She wasn't just venting; this was her way of processing the hole her husband left behind. He was the kind of man who gave himself completely, so others could live in peace. In my book, that made him the kind of soul the world seldom deserved.

"I know you'll miss him, Shanti," I said gently. "Hell, we all will. But you know as well as I do, he wouldn't want you drowning in sadness. He gave his life to make sure you had something more – a chance to live differently, without looking over your shoulder. That's the biggest gift he could've given you."

She pulled the hood of her Dior jacket over her head, her eyes searching me like she was trying to decide if my words were enough to anchor her. Finally, she nodded, her movement slow but deliberate.

"So, what are you even doing here?" she asked, her voice still heavy, as she glanced between me and JoJo, her curiosity cutting through the sorrow just for a moment.

I took a second to think over my response, making sure my words carried the weight of my conviction.

"Rude Boy's death won't be for nothing," I said firmly. "This mess in Atlanta cost him his life. Those issues slowed us down, and Zeus and his people left him to die like he didn't matter. I won't let that slide. I owe it to him to make sure he's avenged." I gestured to JoJo at my side. "And I know JoJo's with me on that."

She stared at me for a moment, her expression caught in a mix of disbelief and acceptance. "You really think you're gonna take a swing at Zeus and his crew for leaving Rude Boy in the dirt, just like that?" she asked bitterly. "My husband…" Her voice caught, and she glanced at the tombstone. She sucked in a sharp breath before continuing. "My husband is gone. Everything he stood for, the reason those niggas get to breathe easy, is because of him. And now he's gone." She paused, looking down at the grave like she was searching for some kind of strength in the words etched there. "Well, I guess it is what it is."

I leaned down, running my hand over the grass in front of the tombstone. "So, what's next for you?" I asked her.

"I don't know," she said quietly. "I might just record my music and travel a bit. But I'm done with this city. The minute I know what's next, I'm getting the hell out."

I smiled faintly, wishing her all the blessings she deserved in my mind. Rude Boy's final wish was to make sure Shanti was safe, and that wish had been fulfilled. She was breathing, standing, and figuring out how to move forward. That was the best we could ask for.

"I guess this is it then," I said as I straightened up. "Goodbye for now, Shanti. I wish you the best of everything."

"Thanks," she said, her voice soft but sincere, before walking away. Her silhouette receded into the distance, leaving JoJo and me in the quiet company of the grave.

JoJo turned to me, curiosity flickering across his face. "So, what's the plan now?"

I didn't look at him immediately. Instead, I gazed at the sky, the breeze tugging at my hair. "Just like I said," I replied after a long pause, "Rude Boy didn't die for nothing. But Zeus thinks he did. Those New York issues? They're far from over. I think we should blow off a little steam first though — take a breather. But make no mistake, I'm not planning to let the Feds catch me in this lifetime. Not now, not ever." I glanced at him with a faint smirk. "We've got lives to fuck up and a long road ahead. Let's see where the crime life takes us, yeah?"

JoJo's lips curved into a small grin, his amusement simmering under the surface. "Sounds like a plan. New York it is…"

And just like that, we stepped forward into whatever storm awaited us, the wind at our backs, and a shared purpose fueling our fire.

The End…

Did you enjoy the read?
Let us know how much by leaving
us a review on Amazon.

IN The Streetz

By: Tron Hill

"That's it right there," Ace mumbled to Whiteboy as vivid images from the first time he'd visited this place flashed through his mind. There was no way in hell he'd managed to avoid the memory of the heinous acts committed here a few years ago. Many days and a few nights he had.

But now, he was back. The past refused to remain at the end of the train of less gruesome thoughts. His eyes lingered another moment. He wished that he hadn't come here before or that his visit had been for another purpose besides the agenda executed that night.

Ace understood that his first time here was due to him being an ignorant part of the hand delivering that fatal coup de grace to the thin line of his blood. Yet he knew that the blame would find no better rightful resting place than the palms of his hands, no matter how often he attempted to lay the fault at the doorsteps of those who puppeteered it.

Mountains of regret spoke from the deeply embedded footsteps he'd taken the last time. Revenge would speak from the ones he was about to take tonight. Hopefully, they'd amend his previous atrocious actions.

Resentment heightened as he stared at the house through the night's shadow. Everything inside of him wanted to explode, and he was more than determined to let it, though only in the faces of those responsible. Tonight would be a new beginning as it had been years ago. However, the difference between then and now was the personal element involved.

"Ace… Ace," repeated Whiteboy until Ace craned his neck toward him. Something roamed within the midst of his eyes, a thing Whiteboy had never seen in his best friend before. He could more than understand though, especially after remembering what Ace had told him about this place.

"Yeah," Ace finally uttered, wanting to stay focused on the task.

"How are you trying to handle this?" Whiteboy peered through the front then out of the back windows of the Suburban, making sure they were in the clear to make whatever movie Ace had in mind.

"See that tree in front of the house?" Ace pointed toward the dimly lit yard directly across from them. "We gonna tie homie to it."

He then turned back toward the house as Whiteboy said, "Say no more."

Opening the driver's door, Ace stepped onto the wet pavement, skimming the entire area. Seeing nothing, he silently closed it. His muted action had been in vain. On the other side of the SUV, Whiteboy had slammed his. The loud bang was what Ace was hoping to avoid.

The last thing he needed was to alert nearby neighbors. "Stupid ass..." he grumbled sotto voce, meeting his careless protégé at the rear. "Let's wake the whole damn neighborhood then."

"Huh?" Whiteboy returned, dumbfounded. Ace could only shake his head, reminding himself that this was Whiteboy he was dealing with. After glancing over the scenery again, he pulled both rear doors open. Instantly, his gaze fell upon their unconscious, hogtied hostage.

"The fuck?" Whiteboy chuckled unbelievingly. "I know this nigga not sleep!" Ace smirked, amazed as well. The dude was on the verge of experiencing death, and all he thought to do was nap. His smirk stretched into a smile.

"How bout I wake him?" Grasping the crowbar stealthily from the floorboard of the Suburban, he raised it then forcefully slammed it down onto the dude's shoulder blade. The guy woke in severe pain. Luckily, the duct tape had secured his mouth because he probably would have awakened the whole damn street from the sound made.

Ace stared down into the tormented eyes, barely able to catch the man's pupils through the darkness. Yet he didn't have to see them to know that an unspeakable fear lay within. And it had every right to be there. If anybody knew the horrid damage Ace was capable of causing, it would be this very person. He'd taught and groomed the young adolescent in all his ways of killing people. And now it was his turn to feel the wrath of his creation.

"How you?" Ace sneered, his lips cracking into a slight grin. "It's time, nigga..." Grabbing him, Ace tugged him toward the edge and over, letting him collide chest first onto the concrete below.

"What? You gonna carry him over there?" asked Whiteboy before snatching up the chains. Surely, he knew the dude wouldn't be able to walk after the beating they'd given his legs only hours ago.

"Nah." Ace knelt, cutting the zip ties which connected his arms and legs. "We gonna drag 'em over there." Gripping him under his armpits without hesitation, the two towed him through the night. His legs slid along, emitting the sounds of leather and gravel frictioning as they continued toward their destination.

Stopping in the darkened yard, they dropped him before the tree. Quickly, Whiteboy began looping the chain around the trunk. Ace lifted the dude from the ground, throwing him hard against the wood. Immediately, Whiteboy secured him to the tree.

Ace fished the blade from his pocket. The man wiggled a little at the sight of the glistening metal, but his movement was weak because resignation had set in hours ago. He knew he would be dying tonight. The how was something his mind hadn't grasped though. He could only hope it would be quick and soon.

Ace placed the knife at the side of his face then slowly inched it down his cheek, cutting both tape and flesh. The guy winced in pain but quickly recovered.

Ace noted his *pretending to be brave* act and smiled while snatching the bloodied strip away, uncovering his mouth. "Agh!" he let out, quickly replacing his cry with a terrible chuckle. "Ace," he began. "You think you gonna get away with this shit, nigga?" The guy grinned, shaking his head slightly. "Nawl... hell nawl. You gonna be in this same position real muthafucking soon. And guess what? I want you to think about me every second death eats at your soul, bitch!"

Ace's smile stretched farther across his face. *And to think this fool would break and beg for what was left of his life. At least some of it.* This had been one of the feats Ace admired about him.

No matter the situation or circumstances, he refused to fold or bend under any kind of pressure — something he embedded in all of them. However, tonight's objective wasn't about breaking him to the point of cowardice. Instead, he would be used as a fatal message.

"Yeah, I'll think about you while I'm offing the rest of them niggas. So, in the meantime, how bout you be death's main course?" Ace pulled the Ruger .45 from his waistline. He glared at his soon-to-be victim, wondering if he knew where they were. If not, then what a perfect time to show him.

"Look..." he said, aiming the pistol at the house.

Reluctantly, the dude craned his neck. At first, he didn't recognize it due to the obscured shadow which covered the entire area. Then, there were a couple of focused moments. And finally, with a few prisms of light from the streetlights, a vivid recollection of the past sprung to the forefront of his mind.

A small chuckle escaped his mouth. "So, you mad?"

Swift and brutally, Ace slapped him with the gun, transforming his giggle into a shriek of pain. "Nah, I ain't mad," Ace calmly retorted. Yet, on the inside, he was burning with rage. The quorum of secrets within some of them was more than evident now. "A little disappointed, *maybe*, but not mad. I'm just going to make all y'all niggas feel the same thing they felt," he finished, clutching the pistol tighter, ready to make the first example.

Disgustingly, the dude spit blood from his mouth, hitting Ace square in the chest. "What they felt? *Ha!* You should know since you are the one that did it to them. You the one, remember? So, kill your muthafucking self, nigga!"

"Nah," Ace snarled, "I prefer you." Those were the last words the dude would hear. The sight of the Ruger found the center of his forehead. The corner of Ace's mouth inched upward as he made sure the discharge would be the last light homie witnessed.

CHAPTER 1: YEARS BEFORE

Ace grew up on the east side of Atlanta, within the confines of a hood called Edgewood — the gutter part of the conservative side of the city. Or at least that was how he always felt. His home consisted of him, his mother, Missy, and his uncle, Mike.

Missy was the boss, the breadwinner who worked a nine to five and a side hustle to ensure her house was a home if nothing else. She made sure every bill was paid and every stomach was filled, no matter what it took. Missy was the true definition of a go-getter. She was one who nevertheless would have been labeled a *real street nigga* had she been a man.

She knew the jungle *ins* and *outs* like the back of her hand. She knew how to handle herself in any situation, regardless of how gangsta things had to get. But you would have easily thought she was an *up-and-coming* actress or runway model if you didn't know her — all thanks to her appearance.

Missy was one of the most beautiful females a guy could lay eyes on. Her skin was a flawless canopy of milk chocolate, resembling one of the chocolate candy Easter bunnies, which was the only reason most people ever thought about the holiday. Her physique… Well, Ace refused to look at his mother like that, but she wasn't anything you'd think to see in projects like the one they lived in.

Uncle Mike, on the other hand, well, he was a whole other story. He always matched the environments he ventured to and hung around the most: smokers, junkies, street corners, and alleys. The only time Ace actually saw him clean himself up was at his grandfather's funeral. Uncle Mike was aight though. The only thing that Ace hated about him was when he'd come home from one of his crack adventures and eat up the whole damn house. Besides that, Uncle Mike was the coolest dude living.

Ace's father, he never knew nor met but he easily figured he looked like him because his skin complexion was more than a few shades lighter than his mother's. Plus Missy sometimes said he favored him, though never explained who *he* was nor ever told him his name. And she really didn't have to because Ace could never think of one reason why he'd want to know, especially after she told him about how he used to beat her up and treat her until she finally got tired of it and left. Constantly, she'd remind her child that it was *fuck him*, which usually ended the conversation about him.

Family was another thing his mother failed to mention. So, basically, Missy and Uncle Mike were all he had and needed. Of the two, Missy had taught him the most about the street life and how to survive if he ever had to. She understood how cruel the game could be and made more than sure that he did too.

Often, she would reiterate, "Baby, get you — you cause ain't nobody gonna do for you like you. And never settle for small shit. Once you do, you always will." Those words, he vowed, were ones he'd stick with until death.

By the age of thirteen, Ace had dropped out of school to chase a career in selling dope. His young mind couldn't conjure a logical reason in continuing his education. The exchange of product for money itself added up to easier somethings than a place which offered a bunch of difficult to understand nothings. To him, school was nothing outside of someone telling you to do something just so you'd end up with, more or less, nothing.

Uncle Mike and Missy had graduated with, she always claimed, *flying colors.* Yet that didn't prevent him from seeing where they had ended up in life with diplomas. She had a son she could barely take care of, and Uncle Mike had a habit he couldn't support or control.

Neither possessed a career, nor financial stability, or anything close to it. All of which motivated the youngsta to follow his ambition of making it as a street nigga. So, he was extra glad and grateful for the day when his fate was finally decided.

Missy had given him an ultimatum, saying, "Either you give the school thing your all and graduate like I want you to do or you give this street life everything you got cause you gonna need it to survive it."

Ace's mind had been made up since the first time his eyes fell upon a little money the fast way. Though he thought better of it — for Missy's sake — to at least pretend he was really giving the ultimatum some thought. *Weighing his options*, he guessed. But the entire time he was *weighing* her words, a phrase was constantly repeating itself in the forefront of his mind — books and bullshit or money and good shit?

So, there you had it. Ace was working his way toward becoming Atlanta's very own Big Meech. The A's Meech...

He smiled at the thought, counting the bread he'd made for Missy. Every now and then, he glanced at the local everyday dudes throwing a football around like that was all their lives consisted of, pretending to be NFL stars they'd never even had the chance to be close to. Neither them or their friends.

And speaking of friends, Ace had none, thanks to Missy's reminding him that, "Friends will kill you, and trust will too. So, fuck friends and trust nothing. I'm your only friend."

His mother felt the need to instill in him the fundamentals of being loyal. She constantly reminded him never to bite the hand that fed him. Well, unless that hand stopped or started pitching crumbs. Yet even so, she continuously ingrained in him that loyalty went deeper than love because loyalty was emotionless.

Missy believed emotions could bring about two results: getting you killed or driving you the fuck crazy. Those were all he needed to know to stay far away from it if he could help it.

Three hundred was the number of the day, riding shotgun in his pocket. He smiled, feeling all bigheaded about the bank he'd made before the end of the a.m.

Missy going to be really happy, he thought, walking into the Red store. The store was small and contained a few crackheads, a couple of nobodies, and a dude at the gambling machine located at the back. From the short distance, Ace figured the dude was a little too young to be chancing what his parents probably provided him with for junk food. But he doubted he'd be on there if he didn't know what he was doing.

Grabbing a drink from the cooler, Ace hopped at the end of the line. A few minutes later, he reached the counter. Wanting to flex a little bit, he smoothly pulled out the stack of bills and removed a ten from the bundle. Then, out of his peripheral, he noticed the young dude who'd been at the gambling machine now thirstily drooling over his shoulder with the world's most gigantic moon eyes locked on the stack of greenbacks.

"Aye… all that's yours?" the young looker asked curiously as Ace craned back a little to get a good look at him.

Nonchalantly, Ace replied, "Yeah."

Quickly, he reminded himself of what Missy said about questions. "A question is always a route to too much information. And if you're going to be in this life, never let anybody know what you know. Cause if you do, you've given them the advantage of knowing more than you."

Ace turned his attention back toward the Arab, who was handing him back two dollars and some change. "Good looking." Ace nodded, accepting the money.

"Aye, shawty… Man, you know homie cheating you, right? The nigga owes you more than that," the young dude told him a little too loudly in his ear.

Ace stood there, stunned a bit by the ringing in his ear and the confusion crowding his mind. Math hadn't been one of his best traits when he did attend school. Nonetheless, he knew what to get for the dope he sold. And Missy had told him that much.

"What?" he finally uttered, dumbfounded.

The young dude stared at him with an arched brow. "Man, this funny looking ass nigga cheating you. You gave him a ten for a dollar drink, and he gave you back two."

Ace glanced down at his hand then at the foreigner glaring at them both. "Get out!" the angry man growled.

Without hesitation, the young dude growled back, "Hell nawl! Cheating muthafucka, give shawty his money."

"Get out now!" the Arab screamed, pointing a finger at the door.

Looking at Ace, the young guy said, "Shawty, you standing there like you just gonna let him take your money."

Stiff, Ace wondered why he hadn't peeped it and why he hadn't said anything still. Then, his eyes lifted to the Arab. "Give me my money." His voice sounded like he was a little boy, asking for something he couldn't have.

Appearing more agitated, the man stormed from behind the counter. He now looked a lot bigger than he seemed a moment or two ago.

Ace, whose body remained rigid, couldn't think of anything to do. His mind was too caught up in grasping the magnitude of the mammoth before him.

As the huge, grumbling man approached, the young dude quickly jumped in front of Ace for the confrontation. "Give him his money!" he barked bravely, yet he looked like an ant compared to the giant.

The Arab's expression became furious, either by the remark or the fact that the young dude wouldn't cower. Void of any hesitation, the big man quickly cocked his hand back. He slapped his little adversary hard across the face, causing him to stumble backward right into Ace.

Shocked by the sudden assault, Ace found it harder to make an attempt to move, thinking, *Damn, this nigga finna slap me too.*

Holding his face, the young guy became motionless. Ace wondered what was going through his young mind, but it was probably nothing because a slap like that most likely knocked every last thought out. But then, he slid a hand to the lower part of his back, pulling something from under his shirt, which turned out to be a small gun.

Wasting no time, the young guy swung it around for the Arab to see his big mistake. Ace was astounded that a gun came out and that someone around his age was handling it like an adult. The only pistols he'd ever seen had been Missy's and the ones on TV. Now though, the one in front of him was taking aim.

The Arab didn't seem one bit afraid. He immediately reached for it and failed to grab it before gunfire sounded throughout the store.

BOOM! BOOM!

The blasts sounded like thunder in Ace's ears. Paralyzed, he watched as the mammoth stumbled two steps backward, staring down at his chest, unbelieving that he'd been shot. However, the two red dots that quickly began to expand throughout the fabric of his shirt made him a believer.

BOOM! BOOM!

Two more shots erupted from the pistol. Ace stared as the slugs forced the big man back into the cooler's glass door before he slid to the floor. The Arab's face contorted into a mixture of anger and sorrow. His chest heaved up and down to the twitch of his body.

Immobile, Ace's retinas mooned at the bloody sight a few feet away from him. Never had he witnessed a murder before in his young life, fourteen years of life to be exact. Of course he'd heard about it. Hell, everybody heard about niggas getting gunned down. But never — ever — had he thought he'd actually see one firsthand.

Lost in his own world, Ace hadn't noticed the movement of the young dude, who was now behind the counter, mashing the buttons of the cash register. If it wasn't for the *beeping* sound he kept hearing, he wouldn't have known that reality was continuing to run its course.

Ace's eyes strayed to the right. *Damn, he fast,* he told himself, watching him press away in urgency. A few seconds later, the register clicked open. Speedily, the young guy snatched at what seemed to be everything. This was amazement number two. Not only had he killed the Arab, but he was now robbing the place.

The young dude moved from behind the counter to the store's door like nothing had happened. Then, cracking it open slightly, he took a peek out.

Still in the same spot, Ace watched him closely, trying to figure out how easy it was for someone his age to take a life and move as if nothing had happened. But then again, how was it so easy for a person to become so unalive?

"Come on, man! What the fuck are you doing?" Ace heard him ask. He was trying to shake the numbness which took hold of his body. Another second would pass before he found the nerve to move, quickly hopping over the dead man's legs.

Stepping out, the dude elbowed Ace slightly, saying, "Play it cool. We good."

Ace prayed like hell they were because any sight of twelve would cause him to shit himself right then and there.

The two of them walked along the sidewalk in silence, both wrapped in their own separate thoughts.

Ace wondered what time their faces would be on the news. Surely someone or something had seen dude — or rather both of them. Too many times before on TV, he'd seen how people committed crimes, thinking that no one had seen them when, all along, someone was watching, waiting to use what they saw to help their own situation in some way.

"Aye, man, you gonna say something or what?" the young shooter finally asked, breaking the irritating quietness between them.

"Like what?" Ace responded, now musing over what existed for them to talk about after dude more than likely made them America's most wanted.

"They call me Whiteboy, shawty."

Whiteboy's complexion defined his name perfectly. He was one of the lightest dudes Ace had ever seen rocking dreads. His features put you in the mind of Kid from the movie *House Party*. Yet, unlike Kid, at fifteen, Whiteboy had wreaked havoc on his peers, something that earned him the title of *teenage beast*.

He was known for knocking out almost all of the neighborhood kids, including a few teenagers and a couple guys older than they were.

Though that was just for starters. Nowadays, he felt the urge to terrorize the nobodies of the projects. Well, that was as long as whatever he did wasn't fucking up certain hustler's money. Yet, then again, what did it matter to him? Who would know that *he* was messing up their paper when no one saw him?

So pretty much, he did what he wanted to, when he wanted to. And he refused to take shit from anybody except his mom and dad, whenever they were back on Earth.

"I'm Ace," Ace returned, glancing around suspiciously. He just knew, at any moment now, the police were going to surround them and probably shoot both of them.

"You stay over here, shawty?"

"Yeah."

"Where bout?" asked Whiteboy, taking a look over his shoulder to make sure no one was following them.

"Over on Macklone Street." Ace had to ask himself, *Why in the hell am I telling him anything?* He hadn't known him a full hour yet, and here he was, letting him know where him and his mother laid their heads. Though he did help him, he guessed.

"You talking about the dead end?"

Reluctantly, Ace nodded his head.

"Oh, I ain't never seen you before. But anyway, I ain't got nowhere to split dis…" Whiteboy said, gripping the bulge of his pocket. "So, let's push to your spot since it's closer." He gazed over what he could see of the street again, more than ready to clear it. And the sooner the better because eventually, the police would be heating up the strip.

What in the world is he talking about? Ace began to think, staring at him, bewildered. The last thing he wanted, or rather needed, to do was take this fool to his house — Missy's house. He had just killed a guy and robbed the Red store, taking Ace with him as he made his escape. Now, he was telling him they were going to his spot to *split* whatever it was. He wasn't that green to not know what he was referring to. The *why* was what he couldn't wrap his mind around. But he knew he'd feel safer at his own home. Plus, his house was only a street over.

"Aight," he finally huffed, hoping he wouldn't regret it.

Walking up Hardee seemed like it was taking forever for the two of them. And after a few more long minutes, they made it to the porch where both collapsed onto the front steps. Wasting no time in pulling out the loot, Whiteboy began counting as if he'd been a cashier before.

Putting some distance between them, Ace sat quietly. Eyeing him, he figured he had to be messed up in the head to be acting as though nothing fatally drastic occurred for that paper. But didn't he have to be crazy as well? He'd brought him to his home to bust down the bread from the murder. Missy was going to kill him.

"Two hundred and thirty-six dollars," Whiteboy said after finishing. Then, he began to thumb through it again.

"Why are you counting it again?" Ace questioned, anxious for him to pocket the money and dip.

With an arched eyebrow, Whiteboy looked over. "I got to give you your cut, don't I?" Then. a smile stretched across his face.

Even though he somehow knew what the dude had in mind, it still was the last thing he expected. Why was he offering him any type of *cut*?

"For what? I didn't do nothing... Nothing but watch." Ace told him, praying that he would just keep it and push before Missy pulled up and caught this strange little nigga counting money on her porch. Conclusions would be jumped immediately, giving their arguments an actual motive for the next few days.

Whiteboy's eyebrow inched up a little more. "Man, you not gonna tell on me, are you, shawty?"

"Nigga, what I look like? Ain't no snitch," Ace shot back, feeling more than a little disrespected. Too many times, Missy stressed that there was nothing in the streets worse than a rat ass nigga.

Often, she voiced that rats were the worst kind of people because they held no loyalty or love for anybody but themselves. Therefore, that made them capable of doing anything, at any given time, to anyone. To her and every other street nigga, they would be killed wherever found or worse. His young mind couldn't even think of something worse than death. And if there was, he most definitely wanted no part of it.

"Just making sure," Whiteboy retorted with a smirk. He liked the way Ace reacted. That let him know they had something in common besides their age bracket. Focusing back on the greenbacks, he began counting again. A few numbers later, Whiteboy extended toward Ace what appeared to be half. In his mind, this would hopefully bring about the beginning of their new partnership.

Hesitantly, Ace took it. *How stupid would it be not to take it?* he wondered. "I still didn't do anything, shawty," he reminded him — and himself.

"Man, I know. But the way I see it, since I helped you out with fat bastard and gave you half the fetty — *for no reason* — since you didn't do *shit*..." Whiteboy emphasized then continued, very focused on Ace. "Maybe you'd fuck wit me, bra."

Ace was lost now. *Fuck wit him? What was he talking about?* There was nothing he could *fuck wit him* on, he knew. "What you mean?" he asked with furrowed brows, wanting to see where this was going.

"Shhh, show me how to get money, like what you carrying in ya pocket."

"Looks like you good doing what you just did."

"What? Man, hell nawl! This is some lil money. Plus that was my first time doing some shit like that." Whiteboy chuckled, actually more surprised that he'd done it than Ace appeared to be. He had to salute himself for crossing a line he'd never thought about traveling and doing it as well as he had.

"What?" Ace's mouth fell wide open in shock. This white dude was crazy for real.

"Yeah. I just did what I saw on *Menace II Society*. You saw it before?"

This nigga got to be crazy, Ace thought, deciding to give him back the money. There was no way he could *fuck wit him* on something that wasn't even his.

"What?" questioned Whiteboy, not understanding why he was shoving the bread back toward him.

"I can't take it," Ace stated, clearly knowing why he couldn't.

"Huh? Why not?"

"Cause..." Ace began rubbing the side of his face. "I can't turn you on to this," he said, gripping the pocket with Missy's money in it.

Whiteboy's expression contorted into one of perplexity. "Why? What, you want to keep it all to yourself?"

"I wish, nigga...It isn't like that though. I just can't." Ace assured him. There was no way in hell Missy would approve of what he was insisting. He could already hear the words that surely would come, trying to let somebody in on her paper. *"Ace, have you lost your fucking mind?!"*

"Look right, bro, I'm a loyal ass nigga. I just want to eat; that's all, shawty." Whiteboy told him, tired of seeing the *haves* enjoy life while he looked bummed out, having nothing to enjoy besides the luxury of his very own imagination.

Ace stared at him as only one of the words he enunciated continued to resonate throughout the interior of his mind. In Missy's words, "Loyalty is the only real thing a nigga could offer you."

"I'll holla at you later, shawty," Ace finally said, trying to figure out if he was just playing the word for some type of leverage or being honest about it because that was a word Missy cherished more than any other and ensured he did as well.

Appearing a little disappointed, Whiteboy gazed out aimlessly toward the street. "Well, look, bra, just think about it." He hoped he would because he more than needed it.

"Yeah..." Ace retorted, giving him some dap then watching him stretch before walking off.

He wasn't even out the driveway when he turned around and sternly fixated his eyes on Ace.

"Say, shawty…" He paused as though he were carefully choosing his next words. "We make a good team together, my nigga. And for some crazy reason, I like you. No homo though." He smiled, proceeding on his way.

Minutes later, Ace still sat on the porch. He replayed everything from the time he'd stepped into the store until the moment the young crazy dude *Whiteboy* introduced himself into his life. Who would have ever seen this happening today? Not him.

Eight o'clock came around. Ace watched as Missy pulled into the driveway. *Dang, I sat out here that long?* he thought, coming to his feet as she opened the car door.

"Hey, baby," his mother exclaimed happily, meeting him at the trunk of the vehicle.

"Hey," he returned tiredly, trying to shake the numbness from his legs.

Missy looked him over once then again. Her expression turned into one of concern. "What's wrong?"

"Nothing..."

"You got the money, right?" she boldly asked with arched eyebrows.

"Yeah, it's right here. Why?" Ace smartly let out. He hated the way Missy looked at him when she thought he'd messed something up.

"Nigga, who the fuck you think you talking to, huh?" She checked him, grabbing his chin with a firm grip.

"N-nobody," he quickly answered. He then asked once she released his face, "Did you bring something to eat?"

"What do you think? When have I ever not brought some home to eat, Ace?" She eyed her son over again, trying to figure out what was wrong with him. It wasn't like him to be with all the extra stuff.

"Well, the money's right here, and everything good." He told her, handing her the paper, hoping it would free him from that stare he hated.

"Alright, get the food from the backseat while I grab the stuff. The police are everywhere. I don't know what's going on."

Ace knew. The big dead Arab crept to the forefront of his mind.

"These niggas getting crazier," Missy shook her head, "and crazier by the day. That's why, hopefully soon, we'll have enough money to move out of this shit hole and somewhere safer and perfect for us." They both shot each other a glance that said *hopefully* because they had heard those exact same words many times before.

Missy, over the years, had matured as a young mother and had acquired big dreams for her and Ace but knew they were far-fetched, especially in their situation. It didn't matter though. She would always want a better life for them without the game or the stress and effects of poverty.

Often, she found herself wondering what life would be like without the struggles and worries of the ghetto. It was life almost impossible to comprehend.

.   .   .

An hour later, they sat at the kitchen table eating Burger King, which they considered dinner damn near every night besides Sundays, the only day Missy cared to put her cooking skills down.

Missy was counting the money when Ace found the courage, feeling the time had come to ask her what he'd thought about since he'd left the convenience store. It took a while to build up his confidence and nerves, but now, he sat there staring at her, ready to get it out, caring less at this point how it would sound coming from his mouth.

Here goes nothing, he told himself before uttering one word. "Missy, I need a gun." He mouthed it boldly, praying she'd understand, yet deep down, he knew she wouldn't. How could she? Her only child was asking for a pistol.

"What?" She looked as if he'd spoken another language. "What?" Her voice became more demanding. "What you just say?" Her eyes bore into him deeply, causing his soul to shiver a bit.

"I-I need a gun," he stated sullenly.

"A gun? For what, Ace?" She tried her best to remain calm, but it was not working for her.

Witnessing her reaction, Ace saw no need to say anything else. Her facial expression let him know that he could be paying the dead Arab a personal visit at any given moment, wherever he was.

"Ace, what the fuck you need a gun for, huh?" she asked, staring daggers into him, honestly not wanting an answer though needing one. Her baby was asking for an instrument she knew he would need and eventually have. It came with the game, but damn, did it have to be so soon?

"For… for protection," Ace reluctantly muttered. He knew she wouldn't let up unless he gave her a reason.

"Ace, did something happen today? And don't fucking lie to me," she growled, poking her index finger at him.

"No..."

"Well, why in the hell do you want a gun fo?" She felt, rather sensed, that there existed something he was purposely trying to avoid telling her. This was only infuriating her more. Her face said it all.

Ace sat there, silent and dumbfounded, now hating that he'd

brought it up. But why wouldn't he? *It came with the life, didn't it? Isn't it a part of the street shit? Isn't it the same reason she kept one?*

Without uttering another word, Missy sprung from the table and stormed out of the kitchen.

"Damn, my stupid ass just had to say something," he whispered to himself, feeling bad about upsetting his mother.

Aggressively, she stomped back into the kitchen with her gun in hand. Missy slammed it down in front of him, causing the table to tremble from the impact. The Glock nine seemed bigger than when he'd snuck a peek at it.

"There you go. Now, what you gonna do with it, Ace?" She glared at him as if his next words had better make more sense than the last ones which fell from his mouth.

Words, he had none. He could only gaze up at her, thinking of how he'd really caused Missy to lose her mind with his dumbass question.

"Well, take it, Ace. It's yours. That's what you wanted, right? Since you want to be a big man and handle whatever it is yourself, besides telling your mother the problem." With each word, it seemed as though a tear readily spewed from the webs of her eyes. One by one, they trickled down her face, staying in tune with every pronunciation from her lips.

"Ace... I'm... I can't no more. You gonna have to figure out how to be a man on your own. . .I can't. I got to wash my hands with you."

There weren't enough words that his young mind could summon, in enough time, to undo the predicament caused by his own urgency. So, he sat there motionless, watching as Missy walked off, face cupped in her hands, leaving her words to linger in his ears.

He didn't want to comprehend what she'd said but found it hard not to clearly understand what she'd meant.

Minutes passed as he remained in the same position and chair. Then, Ace dropped his head. Tears ebbed down his face. It was not because he was hurt but because of the pain he felt for Missy. She had loved him until now, and he knew nothing would ever change that or be the same again.

A mother had lost a son, and a child had forfeited a mother's love.

Now, he'd have to stand on his own two feet and walk the road called life by himself.

Taking the pistol into his grasp, Ace looked over it one more time before tucking it and heading toward his unimaginable fate.

Reaching the end of the driveway, he turned around, exactly how Whiteboy had a few hours ago. He needed one last look at the only place he knew as home. Slightly, he shook his head, realizing there existed a possible chance that he would never step foot in it again.

"Ha, ha..." Whiteboy laughed at the Dave Chappelle show, which was his all-time favorite television show. Watching it had become an every night thing before he fell asleep. What else was there for him to do? There wasn't anybody in his house he could relate to on any type of level or in anyway.

His dad, Cateye, understood nothing past being a mechanic and a hardcore drunk and a man who constantly beat the hell out of his wife and son for any dumbass reason he could think of. Then, there was his mother, Angie, who had a reputation for being a dedicated crack addict and the neighborhood fuck bag who'd have sex with anyone as long as Cateye wasn't around. And the wife, like her husband, jumped on her son just because Cateye kicked her ass.

So, it was pretty much apparent why the television became his primary way of escaping the reality of his household.

Just as he began to lay back and relax, an odd popping sound resonated from his window. Startled, Whiteboy jumped off his bed, wondering what was hitting the glass or at least what was causing it. Slowly, he inched toward the windowpane, tugging back the curtain only enough for a peek outside.

Even though Whiteboy had matured beyond his short life, he was still afraid of the dark and the things his imagination told him lurked there. Glancing out, he noticed the silhouette of a small figure standing on top of the garbage can which sat directly under his window. Squinting, he still found it hard to make out who it was. Had it not been for the porch light, he wouldn't have been able to tell if it was human.

Hesitating another moment, he finally eased the window upward, asking lowly, "Who dat?"

"Come outside, man." He automatically recognized the voice.

Whiteboy hurried down the stairs as fast as he could without alerting Satan's angels. The entire way, he wondered how and why the boy, Ace, had shown up at his house at this time of night. *Maybe he came to his senses,* he began to think.

But why come to them this late? There was always tomorrow unless something important forced the unexpected visit.

Making it to the back door, Whiteboy pulled it open as silently as possible. He slid out, leaving a small crack. "What up, Ace?" he greeted him, giving him some dap.

"Nothing really, just came over to see what you were doing," Ace replied, thinking of how crazy that sounded.

"Huh? Man, come on," chuckled Whiteboy. "This late at night? Nigga, how did you even know where I stayed?"

"A jay down the street told me. I told him I was your cousin," he said with a coy smile.

"Oh, yeah? So, why are you out here so late? It's close to ten." Whiteboy stared at him curiously. He could sense that something more was at play.

Ace stood there a second, trying to decide the perfect way to describe his situation. Nothing he thought of could *explain* his predicament besides the truth. "Man, me and Missy got into it tonight. Then, she kicked me out."

"Who's Missy?" asked Whiteboy, not remembering him mentioning the name.

"My mama, nigga. Who you think?"

"For real? Dang, that's messed up. So, what you going to do, shawty?"

Ace shook his head. "Ion know. I ain't got nowhere to go to and nothing besides a few dollars and a strap."

"A strap?" Whiteboy questioned incredulously. "Where did you get it from?"

"Missy gave it to me right before she kicked me out." Ace hoped someone could make sense of it because he damn sure couldn't.

"Hold on, shawty. You telling me your mom gave you a strap then booted you to the curb?" Whiteboy laughed, unable to control himself.

"Man, you laughing. This shit isn't funny, nigga. I don't have no place to go. Not even for tonight." Ace now fully realized the seriousness of his reality.

"Bra, just chill. Look, you can stay over here till we figure something out." Whiteboy told him, at the same time wondering how in the hell he was going to guarantee that.

For the first time since leaving Missy's kitchen, Ace felt there was hope. There was at least some, regardless of how small it was.

"Oh, so your people will let me stay ova here tonight?" he eagerly asked, ready to accept the invitation.

"Hell nawl," Whiteboy let out, causing Ace to look at him, perplexed. "They really hate that I have to be here."

"So, how am I gonna stay ova here, White?" Ace began to mentally prepare himself, once again, for the first ever sleepover on the street.

Stealing a glance over his shoulder, Whiteboy rubbed his palms together. "Shhh, I'm gonna sneak you in for tonight." He smiled as if he was still putting together the rest of his brilliant plan.

Damn. Ace didn't want to be tonight's test dummy, but he knew he'd be exactly that for something much harder if this failed.

But what is there to lose? he reminded himself before asking, "Where am I gonna sleep?"

Whiteboy's smile stretched farther across his face. "In my closet. Nobody ever goes in there."

Ace gave him an expression like, *Be serious, nigga.* "Man, come on, your closet?"

"Boy, yeah. Trust me on this. That thang like Jurassic Park... a world of its own," he finished, making Ace wonder why he would compare his closet to something like that. He eyed him a moment longer, trying to figure out if he even wanted to know.

"Your closet, what?" Ace couldn't help but ask after acknowledging the fact that he'd be in, on, or around whatever existed within it to make him utter something like that.

Whiteboy peeped his dilemma. "Man, it's just dirty as fuck. But aye, it's the safest place I can think of. Plus, it's ten times better than these bummy streets."

"I guess," returned Ace halfheartedly. There was no point in arguing against that. However, he wondered if Whiteboy's plan would work without his people finding out. He began to pray for himself.

"Aight, just follow behind me as quietly as you can. It's going to be ugly if we wake them. We'll both be looking for a cozy lil spot on the street." Whiteboy assured him.

Pushing the door back open, Whiteboy stuck his head in. He listened a few seconds then gestured a hand for Ace to follow suit. Moving laggardly, Ace tried his best to imitate most of Whiteboy's movement. They stealthily paced through what appeared to be a part of them bummy streets Whiteboy had just mentioned.

Ace peered, trying to penetrate deeper into the darkness beyond the dimly lit area they were moving along, seeing that upon first entering, he had easily assumed mountains of all types of stuff were waiting to be trampled over. And there was nothing besides spots of molded food, old candy wrappers, a few bottles, and pieces of other shit he couldn't quite describe. Some of it protruded from under their feet, serpentine-like, into the darker areas of the interior.

As they continued on, Ace tried his best to avoid letting his feet crash down onto anything capable of making his first visit a devastating one.

Finally moving through and up some stairs, they tiptoed a short distance into a medium-sized bedroom. It was one which could have easily been mistaken for the city's small dump.

Yeah, he definitely hit the nail on the head, Ace thought, remembering the description Whiteboy gave of the place. But then again, that might have been an understatement about it resembling Jurassic Park. It was more like *Trarassic Park.*

While Whiteboy secured his bedroom door, Ace glanced around, wanting to know exactly how he'd managed to survive within this pigpen. Stuff was everywhere. Piles of it. From the world's most extensive food wrapper collection to animal bones on the verge of becoming historical artifacts.

Also, tons of clothing was scattered about, most of them dirty as hell, badly praying for a washing machine's attention. Then, there existed things capable of making sewers complete.

"The streets might of been a lil better than this." Ace snickered, keeping his voice low.

"Nigga, go back to 'em then," Whiteboy retorted with a grin. He waited until Ace was through sightseeing then dropped a hand upon his shoulder.

"Bra, tomorrow, we gonna figure out what to do. So, don't stress it, Tony," he said, giving his best impression of an Italian mobster. Then, pivoting him a little, he pointed at the door covered with a bunch of unintelligible stickers and a poster. "But for now, that's your new home."

Damn, why did I have to ask for a gun? Ace wanted to kick himself square in the butt as he sluggardly stepped over to Hell's entrance. He could only imagine what lay beyond door number three, especially after witnessing firsthand the house of doom.

Reluctantly, he twisted and tugged on the knob. As soon as it cracked open, a burst of fumes exploded outward, tearing at his nostrils, forcing him to quickly retreat with a hand over his nose.

"Nigga… Damn! I should have stayed outside," squealed Ace. The smell was already causing his stomach to somersault.

Whiteboy laughed amusingly at his reaction. "It… it takes a few minutes to get used to. You'll be alright. Just deal with it till the morning." His smile spread farther with every passing second.

"Till morning? Man, I might be dead by then." Ace chuckled, inching his way in. Then, not even caring what he'd land on, he let his body collapse on whatever was waiting below.

"See you in the a.m.," Whiteboy uttered before closing the door.

Ace pulled his shirt over his nose, beginning to think about what would happen when the a.m. came. There was no telling messing with Whiteboy, but he was grateful he wouldn't be facing the unknown alone.

After minutes of switching between thinking about tomorrow and rapping 2Pac's *Hail Mary*, Ace finally dozed off into the sleep he thought would never come.

AVAILABLE NOW!!

OTHER BOOKS BY

Urban Aint Dead

Tales 4rm Da Dale
The Hottest Summer Ever
Hittin' Licks For The Holidays: Atlanta
Wet Dreams On Lockdown: The Nurse
How To Publish A Book From Prison
How To Invest In The Stock Market From Prison
First Summer Out With My Prison Bae
By **Elijah R. Freeman**

Despite The Odds
Despite The Odds 2
By **Juhnell Morgan**

Hittaz
Hittaz 2
Hittaz 3
Hittaz 4
Hittaz 5
Hittaz 6
Coldhearted
Coldhearted 2

Coldhearted 3
By **Lou Garden Price, Sr.**

A YN'S Muse For The Summer
Wizdom: Forever Your Gangsta
Charge It To The Game
Charge It To The Game 2
Charge It To The Game 3
A Summer To Remember With My Hitta
Snatched Up By A Hitta
Santa Sent Me A Real One For Christmas
Wet Dreams On Lockdown: The Unit Manager
Thug Me The Right Way 2
Thug Me The Right Way 3
Seizing A Gangsta's Heart For The Summer
Yours For The Taking
Wrapped Up In A Hitta's Love For Christmas
By **Nai**

A Set Up For Revenge
A Set Up For Revenge 2
Wet Dreams On Lockdown: The Librarian
By **Ashley Williams**

Trickin' On A Heaux For Christmas
Homie Hoppin' For The Holidays
Wet Dreams On Lockdown: The Female C.O
Letters Of His Love
By **Telia Teanna**

The State's Witness
The State's Witness 2
The State's Witness 3
This Time Won't You Save Me
This Time Won't You Save Me 2
His Summer Side Piece

A Holiday Heist
Healing The Heart Of A Detroit Gangsta
Summer Vows With A Detroit Gangsta
The Promissory
The Promissory 2
A Gangsta's Last Kiss
By **Kyiris Ashley**

Stuck In The Trenches
Stuck In The Trenches 2
By **Huff Tha Great**

Melted The Heart Of A Menace
Wet Dreams On Lockdown: Lieutenant Grace
By **P. Wise**

Merry Trapmas
By **Mia Sky**

Thug Me The Right Way
By **DiamondATL & Nai**

Wet Dreams On Lockdown: The Counselor
By **Paris Iman**

Wet Dreams On Lockdown: The Male C.O
By **Tamyra Griffin**

Wet Dreams On Lockdown: The Captain
By **TN Jones**

Wet Dreams On Lockdown: The Warden
By **Shawnice**

Atlantastan
Atlantastan 2

By **Chris Green**

IN The Streetz
IN The Streetz 2
IN The Streetz 3
IN The Streetz 4
IN The Streetz 5
By **Tron Hill**

Hittin' Licks For The Holidays: New York
Bandemic
By **Freshh Moneyy**

Coming Soon From
URBAN AINT DEAD

Drill
The Hottest Summer Ever 2
THE G-CODE
Tales 4rm Da Dale 2
How To Build Your Credit From Prison
By **Elijah R. Freeman**

Despite The Odds 3
By **Juhnell Morgan**

A Felon's Promise
By **Nai**

IN The Streetz 6
By **Tron Hill**

Bandemic 2
By Freshh Moneyy

ASSISTED PUBLISHING PACKAGES

Bronze Package

- Includes:
    - Cover Design
    - Editing
    - Formatting/Typesetting
    - Publishing Consultation
    - Price: $400

Silver Package

- Includes:
    - Cover Design
    - Typing
    - Editing
    - One Flyer
    - Formatting/Typesetting
    - Publishing Consultation
    - Price: $725

Gold Package

- Includes:
- Cover Design
- Typing
- Editing
- Proofreading
- Two Flyers
- Formatting/Typesetting
- Copyright Registration
- Publishing Consultation
- Amazon Upload
  - Price: $975

Platinum Package

- Includes:
- All-in-One Bundle: Typing, Editing, Proofreading, Formatting/Typesetting
- Cover Design
- Three Flyers
- Publishing Consultation
- Copyright Registration
- Amazon Setup & Upload
- One Month Promotion
- Amazon Setup/ Upload
  - Price: $1,200

Individual Services

1.Editing Services
   •Proofreading: $100
   •Manuscript Editing:
   •0-60k words: $350
   •Contact for a quote for manuscripts over 60k words.

2.Manuscript Preparation

•Formatting/Typesetting: We will prepare and arrange your book's text and interior for printing.
    •Price: $100

3.Design Services
    •Cover Design: $100 (2 free revisions, any additional revisions will be an additional cost)
    •Promo Flyer: $25
    •Custom Flyer: Contact for quote

4.Distribution Services
    •Amazon KDP Setup: $25
    •Amazon Upload: $25 (if you already have an account but just need us to upload it for you)

5.Other Services
    •Typing: $300 for manuscripts up to 40k words (Contact for quote for longer projects).

    •Copyright Registration: $100 + site registration fees.

U.A.D PROMOTION PACKAGES

<u>Tier 1: The Basics Package</u>

Price: $99

Target Audience: First-time or budget-conscious authors seeking minimal exposure.

Perks:

- Social Media Shoutout: 3 IG Story posts a week for a month.
  - Inclusion in Newsletter: Mention in the "Sponsored Showcase" section with a link to the book.
  - Digital Promo Graphic: A simple branded image featuring the book cover for the author's use (i.e. Available Now flyer)
  - Support Sunday Link In U.A.D FB Group: Book cover and link in Support Sunday post in group (x4)

<u>Tier 2: The Spotlight Package</u>

Price: $199

Target Audience: Authors seeking increased visibility for their release.

Perks:

- Social Media Shoutout: 3 IG Story posts a week for a month.
  - Inclusion in Newsletter: Mention in the "Sponsored Showcase" section with a link to the book.
  - Digital Promo Graphic: A simple branded image featuring the book cover for the author's use (i.e. Available Now flyer)
  - Support Sunday Link In U.A.D FB Group: Book cover and link in Support Sunday post in group (x4)
  - FB Group Promo: Book posted Monday-Friday in over 20 Urban Reader FB Groups for a month.

Tier 3: Maximum Visibility Package

Price: $299

Target Audience: Authors seeking an increased promotional push.

Perks:

- Social Media Shoutout: 3 IG Story posts a week for a month.
  - Inclusion in Newsletter: Mention in the "Sponsored Showcase" section with a link to the book.
  - Digital Promo Graphic: A simple branded image featuring the book cover for the author's use (i.e. Available Now flyer)
  - Custom Quote Graphic: 3 Eye Catching Quote Graphics that can be used on Social Media.

- 3 To 5 Character Visuals: Visuals of the characters in your book that can be used for promo.
- Support Sunday Link In U.A.D FB Group: Book cover and link in Support Sunday post in group (x4)
- FB Group Promo: Book posted Monday-Friday in over 20 Urban Reader FB Groups for a month.
- Paid Ad: We will run an Ad for your book for a month on a Sponsored Showcase page with a customized caption, targeting your book's audience to grow your readership.

BOOKS BY

URBAN AINT DEAD's C.E.O

<u>Elijah R. Freeman</u>

Triggadale 1, 2 & 3

Tales 4rm Da Dale

The Hottest Summer Ever

Murda Was The Case 1, 2 & 3

Hittin' Licks For The Holidays: Atlanta

Wet Dreams On Lockdown: The Nurse

How To Publish A Book From Prison

How To Invest In The Stock Market From Prison

STAY CONNECTED

Follow
Elijah R. Freeman
On Social Media

FB: Elijah R. Freeman
IG: @the_future_of_urban_fiction